THE PARDNERS

THE PARDNERS

George Dalton

ISBN: 0692838236
ISBN 13: 9780692838235

This book is dedicated to the brave men and women who serve faithfully and too often die serving the law and protecting us all.

George is the Arthur of:
A Collision of Dreams
Holding on to the Dream
Coming soon...
Following the dream
The dream series follows Sam McClanton and his family through four generations starting with Sam meeting Mattie Ann. She had a dream getting married when she met the right man., Sam had a dream of getting married in seven or eight years when the ranch was built they had A Collision of Dream.
The Sound of Silence
Starts a new family in a different story.

CHAPTER ONE

A cocky, self-confident young man who had just turned eighteen years old five days ago, sat outside the administrator's office. He held his Stetson hat in his hands, because he had been taught you never wear a hat inside a building. He had no idea why the dean had summoned him to his office. He hadn't done anything recently.

That fight he got into with Tommy Lee would not be that big a deal.

Father O'Malley was a tough school master but a kind man at the same time. In fact, he was the only "father" Grady McCain had ever known since his own dad was killed when he was a baby. Then his mother died when he was three years old and the county sheriff brought him to the boy's ranch, where he grew up. Growing up at an orphanage for boys had been a hard life, but a good one as well. The sisters were strict. The work was hard. Each boy had to share the load for running a self-sustaining ranch.

The young assistant Padre, motioned for him to come into the priest's office. The priest had a sad look in his eyes. Pointing to a straight back wooden chair he said, "Sit down Grady." He looked at Grady for a few seconds without saying a word.

Grady started to feel sweat collecting around his collar. *What is this about?*

"Grady, I have enjoyed watching you grow from a young scrapper that drove the sisters crazy at first, into a fine young man. However, the church is poor here in this part of Texas and we get no funding from the church. We have a waiting list of young orphaned boys waiting to get in. Therefore, we have to send you older boys out to make room for the younger ones waiting to get in. Now that you are eighteen you have reached the age where we have to assume you are a man." The priest reached in his desk and counted out 20 silver dollars. "Grady, it saddens me to see you go and it saddens me that the ranch can't give you more to get started with. Take this and then go to the mess hall and eat lunch. Then pack up your belongings and go to town. I am sure you will find someone who can hire a strapping young man. Stay away from the painted women and out of the gambling halls." The priest did the sign of the cross on the front of his cassock and said, "Go with God, Grady, go with God." His eyes looked extremely sad.

Stunned, Grady stumbled to his feet, it was obvious the meeting was over. The priest motioned to the twenty silver dollars laying on the desk.

Grady felt like he was walking in a fog, even though it was a bright sunny July day in Texas. The temperature would easily reach 100 degrees. His boot heel missed the bottom step as he walked out of the building. He took three quick stumbling steps before he regained his balance. He was now homeless. Where was, he going to sleep tonight? Father O'Malley said go to the mess hall and eat lunch. Walking into the mess hall the sights and smells felt different. He picked up a tray but nothing looked good. He didn't feel like eating.

The sister serving put something on his plate. The other boys were jostling and talking. Grady walked to a table in the corner where no one was sitting. He felt like every boy in the room was staring at him. Just three hours ago, he was eating breakfast here in this room, now he felt like an outsider.

He had to think. The padre said eat, that was a good idea because right now he didn't know where his next meal would come from. Mechanically he spooned bland tasting stuff into his mouth. Think, that is what he needed to do think. It was five miles to town. How was he going to get there in the heat of the day? What was he supposed to do when he got there? Find a job? Where? What kind of job?

Soon the lunch room started to clear out as the boys went back to their chores. Grady walked slowly back to the dorm. Picked up his meager belongings and rolled them in his other shirt and tied a string around the bundle.

He walked out the gate and turned his feet toward the unknown. He had never felt this loneliness before. He couldn't remember his dad and only vaguely remembered his mother. Boy's town was the only home he had known. Then he remembered the padre had always told them they were never really alone, God was always with them. *"Lord I sure feel all alone right now. I sure need you to go with me today. I'll admit I am scared and I sure do feel alone in this big old Texas world*. Right now, I have no family and not one single friend."

A road runner cock popped out of the dried grass alongside the road and ran along in front of him, his first inclination was to shoo it away. Then it occurred to him that this bird was the only friend he had in the entire world.

"Mr. Roadrunner, I don't know where either one of us are going. But I do appreciate your company."

One hour later as they neared the town of Abilene, Texas, they met a wagon going the other way and the roadrunner disappeared into the bushes beside the road. A few minutes later, a hot dusty, thirsty, lonely boy/man walked into the town of Abilene. He didn't own a horse a saddle or a gun.

Grady stopped and stood staring down the main street. The one main street appeared to go on forever. As far as he could see the view looked the same, flat, dry prairie. Not a tree in sight anywhere.

I see they have a watering trough in the street with a pump, I can at least get a drink.

Walking to the trough he took off his hat and splashed water over his head and neck then worked the pump handle until fresh cool well water gushed forth.

"Ah that feels so cool." He let it dribble off his fingers. Cupping his left hand under the stream he worked the pump handle with his right hand and drank from the cup made by the palm of his hand.

Looking around the strange town, Grady saw a sign that said Hotel. *I guess I could go rent me a room until I can figure out what I'm supposed to do to make a living for myself.*

Walking into the hotel the first thing he thought was that it's cooler than out in the sun. Looking around at the polished wood floors and paneled walls, WOW. *A polished hand rail runs all the way to the top of the stairs.*

I wonder who that guys is standing over there behind that counter.

The man was wearing a shiny white shirt and black tie. He said, "Welcome to the Abilene hotel. Do you need a room?"

"Yes sir, I reckon I do. How much is a room?"

"Three dollars a day. How many days are you going to be with us?"

Grady looked hard at the man then said, "Sir, I've been living out at the boy's ranch just about all my life. All I've got is $20.00. Is there any place that I can sleep that's cheaper?"

"You're one of Father O'Malley's boys?"

"Yes sir."

"He gives each one of you boys $20.00. I don't know where he gets that, but he's a good man and does the best he can for you boys. You're a strapping good size, you should be able to find work at one of the ranches here about. You might try old Bledsoe over at the livery stable. He's been known to let one of you boys' sleep in the hayloft."

"Much obliged sir." Grady clamped his hat back on and walked to the livery stable.

A wiry little old man sat on a cane bottom chair in the shade of the barn chewing on a straw. "Are you Mr. Bledsoe?"

"I am."

"Sir I've been living out at Father O'Malley's ranch just about all my life. Today Father O'Malley told me it was time for me to move on and make room for some younger ones needing to come in."

"Gave you $20.00, did he?"

"Yes sir."

"I'll tell you that old padre is a fine fellow. What he does for you boys is the good Lord's work. Every year or so I see one or two of you young fellows come through. Mostly they're good boys or men. If you stay out of them gambling houses and don't spend much time with the painted ladies, you'll do alright."

"That was the last thing Father O'Malley told me."

"Well son what can I do fer ye?"

"That fellow at the hotel said I might could sleep in your hayloft until I can get a riding job somewhere."

Squinting his eyes, he looked at Grady. "I'd say you are about twelve hands tall and you weigh about five and a half stones. So, you're big enough to do a man's work. Let me see those hands."

Grady opened up his hands, palm up and said, "Sir, I don't know what you just said. How tall is twelve hands?"

"Oh, that's horse talk. A horse is so many hands high, a hand is the span of a man's hand when he spreads his fingers out. When you are buying, or selling a horse you reach down to his front hock and spread your fingers up his leg. Then put your other hand above that'en and count how many hands it is to the top of his withers, you know his shoulder. So, I'm guessing if I stood next to you and reached down to your ankle it would be about twelve hands to the top of your head."

"Well how much does a rock weigh?"

"Huh? Oh, you mean a stone. That's an old English term. In the old days when folks didn't have proper scales a stone was about thirty pounds. So, I figure you weigh between one hundred and fifty and one hundred and eighty pounds."

The old man looked at his hands, "Well you've done a sight of work out at the boy's ranch, that's a good thing. Tell you what I'll do, I'm getting down in my get-a-long. This old rheumatism's getting me down. I'll let you sleep in the loft free, if you'll help muck out the stalls every day and throw down the hay for me."

"That's mighty nice of you sir."

"Go on over there to the feed mill and talk to Johnson, tell him you're working for me a little. He may need a little help too. One other thing, boy you stay away from them Higgins boys. They 're big and they're poison mean"

CHAPTER TWO

When Grady walked into the feed mill, the first thing he saw was two big ole boys that together looked like they could lift a freight train right off the tracks. When they stood side by side you would have thought it was night the way they blocked out the sun.

He soon learned, they were the Higgins. Lonnie and Ronnie, Lonnie looked like he was as mean as an old coon with his tail in a trap. Ronnie made him look like a choir boy. Grady had been on the boxing team out at the boys' ranch, but he had never fought anyone as big as either one of these guys. Either one would be a contest.

Grady was looking for a job, he didn't want any trouble, so he ignored them. Walking into the mill he saw a large hopper filling sacks with grain. A fellow was using a big needle to stitch the top of each sack closed and filling another. The guys he assumed were the Higgins were grabbing each filled bag and stacking them in stacks apparently by types of grain.

He saw an office toward the back of the building. Seeing an older man sitting behind a desk working on some ledgers, he tapped politely on the door. "Are you Mr. Johnson?"

The old man laid down his pencil and looked up, "Yes sir, what can I do for ya?"

"I'm looking for a job. Mr. Bledsoe said you might could use some help."

"Are you doing some work for old Bledsoe?"

"Yes sir. He's letting me sleep in his hayloft and I'm to feed the horses and muck out the stalls. That's good but it don't give me any eat'n money."

"You're one of Father O'Malley's boy ain't cha?"

"Yes sir."

"That old hound dog Bledsoe, he's pretty good about helping one of you boys out when he can, but it also gets him free help. Okay, you can start tomorrow. Pays you $2.00 a day. You can lift a hundred-pound sack of corn can't cha."

"Yes sir. By the end of the day I might have to use two hands."

The old man chuckled and said, "We'll see how much spunk you got left in you by quittin time."

As Grady was walking out he heard one of the Higgins say, "Another one of them waifs from the orphanage, probably a bastard kid at that."

The hair on the back of his neck stood up, he started to turn around but out of the corner of his eye he saw that Mr. Johnson was watching him.

Grady looked toward the saloon and thought about going to get a beer, but decided, no I'm not gonna go there. Instead he saw a sign saying May's Café. His stomach growled. I haven't had anything to eat since I left the lunch room.

When he walked in the first thing he saw was a matronly looking lady serving food at one of the tables. When she saw him she said, "Just make yourself at home anywhere, I'll be with you in just a minute."

The food smelled delicious, his stomach growled again. He saw a sign on a chalk board that read biscuits and gravy and coffee twenty five cents.

The lady appeared at his table, "What'll you have sir?"

"I think I'll have some of them biscuits and gravy if you have any left."

"You've got it. Biscuits and gravy coming right up. You're new in town, don't remember seeing you before."

"Yes ma'am. I just got a job working for Mr. Johnson over at the feed mill."

"Johnson's a good man. Just watch yourself around them Higgin's boys."

"That's what I've been told. I'll leave them alone if they'll leave me alone."

As he sat there drinking his coffee he felt pretty good. *You know this morning when I got up I was a kid living at the Boys ranch. Now I have a place to stay, and I've got a job and $20.00 in my pocket, that's a pretty good start. I'll stay there with Mr. Bledsoe and save my money, until I can save enough to buy me a horse and saddle and a gun, then I may just travel around and see me some country.*

The first few days went by in a blur. He was up at first light, got the stalls mucked out, fresh hay down to the horses and walked to May's Café for breakfast. Then it was load 100 pound sacks of feed all day. A quick trip down to the creek to strip off and dive in. Limp home, check the horses and climb up to the hayloft where he collapsed in slumber.

He worked side by side with the Higgins boys all week ignoring their snide remarks. He would show them, he threw one sack of feed for every sack they threw. Each one of them Higgins stood three inches taller and outweighed him by thirty pounds but they couldn't out work him.

Saturday, Mr. Johnson called him into the office and said, "Grady, my boy, I've been watching you all week. You've done a good job. Here's twelve dollars. We don't work on Sunday, if you get drunk tonight and blow all your money don't come whining to me on Monday saying you don't have any eat'n money."

"No sir. I might drink a beer ever now and then but I ain't no drinkin' man."

"That's more than I can say about them two lunk heads." Nodding toward the Higgins boys.

Grady went over to the loft and got his clean clothes still wrapped up in his clean shirt. Went down to the creek and dived in. He always felt better when he got the sweat and feed dust off of him. He then dressed in his clean pants and shirt. Took the clothes had been wearing all week and washed them out. He would take them back and hung them up to dry in one of the empty stalls.

Walking back to town he was thinking *I'll go hang up these wet clothes then I'll go to May's for supper, I'm starving, I might break down and have me one of them fried steaks. Father O'Malley gave me $20.00, I've spent fifty cents a day eat 'en at May's. So that means I've got $17.00 left and Mr. Johnson just gave me $12.00 more. So now I've got almost $30.00. Shoot at this rate in a couple of months I'll have a $100.00. I'll buy me a good horse and a saddle. Then I'll get me a six-shooters.*

Something hard slammed into the back of Grady's head.

Grady felt something wet on his face, he slowly opened his eyes, a dog was licking his face. It was dark, he was lying face down in the dirt and a stray dog licked him in the face again. He tried to sit up and pain racked through him. What happened? His hat was over on the side of the road and when he picked it up he saw that the crown was crushed in. Reaching back he felt a large knot on the back of his head. He reached into his pocket and discovered all of his money was gone. He had been robbed. Somebody had slipped up behind him and whacked him on the head with something and took all his money. Then it dawned on him, he hadn't even eaten supper yet. His stomach growled, now he didn't have any money for supper. If he hadn't been a man he would have sat right there and cried.

He remembered that farmer down there by the creek had some peach trees. He had seen some lying on the ground. He wouldn't take any off the trees but he could get some of them over-ripe ones lying on the ground. It wasn't much but it would be something.

When he started to walk off he looked down and the dog was walking beside him. He said, "Well come on with me, you may be the only friend I've got around here. If you want something to eat you've got to catch it yourself cause, I got nothing to give ya."

When he started to crawl up into the loft he looked down and the dog curled up in the dirt at the foot of the ladder. Grady's head was drumming with pain. When he closed his eyes the barn seemed to be whirling around. He had to open his eyes and stare at the roof beams to make them stand still. The thought occurred to him, what if I die during the night? Will they take me back out to Boy's town and let the padre bury me?

When he opened his eyes again it was getting daylight. The pain had subsided but when he tried to put his hat on he touched the knot and that hurt like the dickens. Slowly he sat up. Well *Grady you can't lay here all day feeling sorry for yourself, you've got chores to do.*

His stomach growled and then it hit him he had the peach tree trots. He barely made it to the outhouse. When he came back into the barn the dog was standing there looking at him as if to say, are you alright? Grady went to the water bucket and drank his fill. The he tipped the bucket so water spilled out for the dog. Grady felt weak, he knew he needed nourishment. He felt in his pockets again, nothing, the robber got it all.

"Well dog what's your name? Where did you come from? Are you somebody's pet? Are they looking for you right now?" Grady looked at the dog, it wasn't a big dog, looked a little like a shepherd mixed with who knows what. What am I gonna call you? I think I'm just gonna call you Knot cause this knot on my noggin is how I got you." He reached over and rubbed the dog's ears. "Well one thing about it, you stood by me when no one else did. I guess you're probably an orphan too so I guess we'll stick together."

"Knot, go find yourself something to eat and while you're at it bring some back for me too."

The dog just tilted his head to one side and looked at him.

Grady looked at the feed corn he was feeding the horses. Then took a hand full and laid it on a flat rock then took another rock and crushed the kernels. He then poured the powder into a dipper of water and drank it. After three cups of water corn-flour mix he felt better. What he really wanted was a cup of coffee. Then he sat there thinking about who could have whacked him on the head and took all his money. The first persons who came to mind was the Higgins. Yet he had no proof that it was them. They were mean and rude, but were they thieves?

Monday morning his headache was gone, the lump on the back of his head still wouldn't allow his hat to fit right. He was hungry... but when he got up to do his chores Knot was right beside him. He did his chores and reported to work at the feed mill. Knot laid down in the shade next to the loading dock.

All day long the Higgins boys talked about all of the steaks they had eaten over the weekend. They bragged about the three eggs they had for breakfast and of course they had steak with their eggs.

Just before quitting time Mr. Johnson called him into his office. May tells me you never came in to eat over the weekend and you didn't stop in for breakfast this morning. Why?"

Grady told him about getting hit over the head and robbed. The old man nodded his head. Then said "You can't work and not eat." He reached into his pocket and pulled out a roll of bills and peeled off three dollars. "Here consider this an advance on this week's pay. You head over to May's and get something to eat."

Grady wanted so say no but about that time his stomach growled again so he took the money. "Thank you sir."

CHAPTER THREE

The week crept by one long day at a time. It wasn't the work that made time drag it was the constant taunts from the Higgins. By Saturday Grady had taken about all he could stand. Mostly it was just words but they were starting to get physical. Nothing big just a shove here a bump there.

They were loading the last load in a wagon. Grady had a hundred pound bag of feed in his hands up over his head getting ready to throw it on the wagon.

Lonnie said "Get out of my way scurvy," and slammed his elbow into Grady's ribs. The pain was intense. Grady didn't say a word.

Mr. Johnson was watching from the door of his office and saw what happened. He thought *they are going to push that boy too far one of these days and those two are going to be in for a surprise.*

Grady dropped the heavy sack over the side board of the wagon and in one fluid motion spun around and slammed all five knuckles on his right hand against the chin of Lonnie Higgins. Lonnie was standing there with a hundred pound bag in his hand and was not expecting anything to happen. One crashing right hand and he hit the deck out cold.

Ronnie was walking up behind his brother with a bag over his massive shoulder. Grady calmly stepped over Lonnie and planted a solid right cross on Ronnie's big bulb of a nose. Ronnie stumbled back and dropped the bag he had on his shoulder. Blood cascaded down his chin and dripped on the front of his sweat stained shirt. He shook his head and looked at his brother lying on the loading dock. Then bellowing like an angry bull he charged Grady his massive fists flying.

Grady ducked under a crushing right but a powerful left smashed into the side of his head, spinning him around. Stars filled his head. Before he could get his vision to clear, Ronnie Higgins slammed a solid right to his ribs. Grady felt a rib break. Blood gushed from a cut on his right ear. Ronnie Higgins waded in beating him savagely on the head and shoulders.

Grady ducked under the raining blows and planted his head on Ronnie's chest. Then slugged him in the stomach three fast hard blows. Ronnie gasped and stepped back. When he did Grady never let him get set again. He stepped forward and whipped a hard right, smashing Ronnie's lips against his teeth, bringing blood. Ronnie Higgins stumbled backward and Grady followed him slashing wicked blows left and right. A cut appeared over Ronnie Higgin's right eye.

When Ronnie brought his hand up to protect his face Grady dropped back down and boomed powerful blows to his stomach. Ronnie Higgins mouth dropped open as he gulped for air. A wicked right caught the jaw hanging open and broke the jaw bone instantly.

Mr. Johnson said, "That's enough Grady. He's whipped."

Lonnie Higgins started to wake up. He moaned and then sat up looking glassy eyed around. Mr. Johnson said, "Get up and take your brother over to see the doc. I suspect he's got a broke jaw."

Doc Baker looked at Ronnie's jaw. "Yep, looks like it's broken. That must have been a heck of a fight. I can set it and wire your teeth shut until it heals but it'll cost you $40.00."

Ronnie motioned for Lonnie to pay the man. Lonnie dug all of the crumpled up money out of his pockets. All he had was $40.00. He said, "Doc if I give you this we won't have nothing left to eat on."

"You should have thought of that before you started a fight."

"We didn't start nothin'. That scurvy kid from the orphanage just hit me on my chin and knocked me out then jumped on Ronnie. When I came to Ronnie was hurtin'. So I brought him over here to see you."

"You two are not only big bullies, you're also lying. Everybody in town knows how you've been pickin' on that boy. Alright give me $37.00 that'll leave you three dollars to eat on till you can get paid again. He ain't going to eat anything, he can't suck through this rubber tube for a while." He handed Lonnie a foot long piece of rubber tubing.

Grady's hand hurt where he had skinned his knuckles and his ear hurt. Yet inside he felt good because he stood up to them. He could feel his hand starting to swell and his ear was swollen. "Come on Knot, let's go soak in the cool creek water for a while."

Grady peeled off his sweat stained clothes and eased into the cold water. He laid back on a large rock slab and allowed the cool refreshing fast running water to sluice over his tired whipped body. *I am not 100% certain that the Higgins were the ones who stole my money but I have taken all of their bullying I'm going to take.*

Knot started to growl a low growl deep in his throat. Quick as a beaver Grady popped out of the water and reached for his clothes. Just then a group of Mexican women stepped through the brush with bundles of clothes they were coming to wash in the stream.

Grady yelled, the women screamed. Knot started barking, you have never seen a man jump into a pair of pants so fast. Grady grabbed his boots and shirt in his hands and raced through the brush back toward the barn. As he scrambled to get away, running barefoot over the rocks and brambles, he felt his face getting hot when he heard the women giggling back by the creek.

Sunday morning Grady decided to amble over to the church, he had nothing else to do. Knot trotted alongside. When they reached the front of the building Grady said, "Knot, you need to wait out here. I don't imagine they allow mongrel dogs in church, in fact, they may not want mongrel boys inside either."

The church was cooler than outside and the singing was easy to listen to. When he started to leave, the preacher was standing at the door shaking people's hand, "I'm Pastor Sullivan, I don't believe I've met you before. Welcome."

Clasping the Pastors outstretched hand Grady said, "Grady McCain. No sir, my first time, I'm new in town. I work for Mr. Johnson over at the feed mill."

The preacher leaned in close so no one could hear what he said next and said, "So you're the one that gave old Ronnie Higgins a whoppin'. He's been needin' it for a long time but watch your back, they're a mean bunch."

As Grady pushed his hat on he happened to look back, and saw the prettiest redhead he had ever seen, in a gorgeous teal green dress, shaking the pastor's hand. He heard the pastor say, "Colleen, nice to see you again today."

Grady and Knot, walked on down to May's for a bit of lunch. Knot curled up on the board walk by the door when Grady went in. Grady was sitting there sipping his coffee when an older man walked in with Colleen by his side. As they sat down at a table across from Grady, a dude in a tan business suit and polished boots stepped through the door. He walked straight to the table where Colleen and the older man sat, Grady assumed he was her father. Without being invited the dude pulled out a chair and sat down. Grady caught a look of disapproval on Colleen's face as the dude sat down.

The dude looked at Colleen and said, "Hello darling."

"I told you not to call me that."

The dude smiled a sleazy smile, "I like feisty women. You'll come around once you get to know me better."

Turning to the older man the dude said, "Look O'Shanity as you know I bought your note from the bank, so you need to tell this red headed daughter of yours she needs to start being a lot nicer to me because you're already behind on the payment."

"Now, look Jud, you leave Colleen out of this. She makes up her own mind who she likes and who she don't. You know we didn't have hardly any rain last year and I couldn't make a trail drive but we have a good crop of young steers this year and I'll pay that darn note in full as soon as we can get a group of drivers to take them to the rail head."

From where Grady sat he saw a look of disgust on the pretty redhead's face, when she looked at the dude.

CHAPTER FOUR

A few days later Grady was sitting in May's eating breakfast when two drummers came in and sat down next to him. He heard one of them say, "At the rate they are laying down rail they're moving that railroad about thirty miles a day. It's amazing to watch those track layers. They have about ten men, five on each side of a flat wagon filled with steel rails. The foreman hollers, *rail* and they slide one rail off each side of the rail car and march forward. He then yells, drop, and clunk down it goes, and a pair of men drop a clamp on the junction of the two rails. Then the horses pulling the rail car rolls forward on the new rail and they drop another one. As soon as the rail car moves forward to the next joint. Then spikers with big hammers step up and drive large spikes into the wooden ties to tie the rail down. It's like watching a band march--- its rail--- drop--- step ---clamp--- hammer, it is something to watch."

"Yeah, we've got to get these right-a-ways signed up because they are in Atlanta today, if they can keep moving thirty miles a day, they'll be here in Abilene, Texas, in less than a month."

"Jud said not to worry about that old man O'Shanity, he had that under control."

"He'd better because that old man's land sets right in the way."

The men laid two quarters on the table and walked out. Grady sat there thinking. Wonder what that was all about. *Who was the old man whose land they wanted? Could they have been talking about Colleen's father? They mentioned some dude named Jud. Could they have been talking about the dude that was so rude to Colleen and her father? Or is there more than one man in town named Jud?*

Colleen looked at her father sitting next to the fireplace. He looked tired and drawn with worry lines on his face. "Dad, it's going to be alright."

"No, darling it's not. I wish I was the man I was ten years ago, I'd fight that smart mouth Jud and whip his sox off. Ever since that horse fell on me I don't have much fight left in me. I've been trying to hang on to this ranch for you and your sister's families someday. If I lose the ranch I've got nothing to leave you and your sister. You're both pretty young women. I can't stand the thought of something happening to me and y'all being left all alone and destitute. They'll attack y'all like a pack of wolves."

She reached over and took her daddy's tired old hand and said, "You're still the best man I've ever known. God always provides a way. You'll figure out a way to pull through this just like you've always done."

"I've been hearing rumors of the railroad coming this way and they'll pay for the right of way to lay tracks on our land. Last I heard they were clear over in Georgia or somewhere the other side of the Mississippi. I had to borrow money to buy supplies since we couldn't make a cattle drive last year. All I owe is a few hundred dollars. I don't know how that Jud got his hands on the note but he claims he bought it from the banker. If that railroad would pay me to run tracks across our land I could pay off that note and then when we made a drive to sell the steers we would be alright."

"You know he told me he would tear up that note if I would marry him."

He turned and stared at his daughter, "Did he actually say that?"

She nodded her head.

He sat quietly for several heart beats then quietly said, "I'm gonna kill that low life fool."

"No daddy. If you kill him they might hang you then where would Marlene and I be?"

CHAPTER FIVE

Sunday morning Grady got up early and saddled a horse Mr. Bledsoe had loaned him. He would not be going to church today. He wanted to get out of town, just to get some fresh air.

Starting out at a trot on the road toward the boy's ranch, he felt a little funny, he had not been out that way since the day he walked away.

He was riding north. Grady watched the sun slowly peek over the ridges to the east. WOW! It was breath takingly beautiful. There was one large tree on the ridge directly between Grady and the rising sun. All around him the blackness of night still shadowed the plants and ground. Yet when he looked toward the east, light filtered through the tree like water, making the tree appear like the burning bush in the Bible. The ground around the base of the tree was a beautiful golden lemon yellow, the sky above the tree morphed from a bright yellow right at the top of the tree, the sky slowly changing to darker and darker shades of silver and blue as his eyes moved up in the sky.

While he was enjoying the beauty of the sunrise he realized he was also listening to a Robin singing clear sweet notes. Looking closer he saw a lone Robin perched in the top branches of the tree silhouetted in the sunrise. The bird was singing his little heart out. He appeared to be waking the morning.

Grady had never seen a sunrise like that one. Maybe it was a good sign. Then his thoughts turned to a beautiful girl with red hair. I wonder how old she is. She is probably twenty or twenty one. Kind-ah old not to be married. Although, as pretty as she is she has probably had plenty of suitors. I sure hope she don't end up marrying that Jud fellow, he seems like a sleaze bag.

Jud strutted into the saloon, just inside the door, he paused a few seconds to allow everyone in the room to notice him. He didn't have on a top coat because it was too hot but he did have on a beautifully tanned doe skin vest, with a big gold watch chain streaming across from his left side to the pocket on his right side. He wore a hand tooled wide leather belt and custom holster for his silver plated pistol with the pearl handle grips. He strolled over to one of the tables and motioned for one of the bar girls to join him. As soon as she walked over he grabbed her around the waist and plopped her down on his lap.

She said, "Jud, if you want someone to sit on your lap you could at least ask."

"Why, in this world should I ask, if I want something I don't ask, I just take."

The two railroad land agents walked into the saloon. When they saw Jud they walked over to his table. He pinched the girl on her bottom and pushed her off his lap, then said, "Darling, I've got to talk some business with these gentlemen. Don't get far, 'cause when we get through talking, I want you back. Don't be going off with nobody else until I get through with you. You understand?"

Before she could answer, he stood and stuck out his hand, "Gentlemen, it's good to see you again. Have you got everything about wrapped up?"

"We've got contracts on every piece of right away between here and Sweetwater except that section through the gap."

"How much are you ending up paying per mile?"

"It started out at ten dollars a mile but the price always goes up when word gets around as to what we're doing. What about that last piece through the gap? Without that we would have to change the whole route."

"Well fellows, that old man is pretty cagey. So that five mile section is gonna cost you a thousand dollars a mile."

"That's ridiculous. I thought you said you had that one under control cause you was gonna marry his daughter."

⊨⊣ ⊢⊨

Colleen brushed her hair until it shined. She was deep in thought. *The idea of allowing that creep Jud to even touch me gives me the shivers. However, I can't stand to see my father like he is now. He's worried sick. I've got mother's old jewelry. I might get $100.00 for it. I hate the thought of selling it, it's all I've got of her. Maybe if I pray about this the Lord will cause something to happen.*

Lord, I don't know how you can help us out in a situation like this but I don't know anywhere else to turn. I don't want to see my daddy lose his ranch. If you want me to marry that Jud fellow, you need to make me stop being so squeamish every time he looks at me with those pig eyes. Lord I don't see anyway out. We need something unexpected to happen.

Amen.

⊨⊣ ⊢⊨

When Grady walked into the mill Ronnie and Lonnie were already there. He didn't know what to expect from them. Lonnie walked over to him and said, "We don't want no hard feelings. You whopped us both fair and square," and stuck out his big hand to shake hands.

Grady looked at Ronnie who looked like he was losing weight on his liquid diet. "What about Ronnie?"

Ronnie mumbled something.

Grady said, "What'd he say."

Lonnie laughed and said, "He said you still have an ugly dog."

Grady laughed and said, "You better not let Knot hear you say that, you may have another fight on your hands."

Ronnie stuck out his hand and mumbled something but Grady couldn't understand anything he was trying to say. Grady was relieved when he shook both their hands. Work went well that whole day. Ronnie was dragging a little by the end of the day, but that was to be expected. He wasn't getting much to eat. They had one hundred pound bags stacked on the dock ready to load and no wagon to load.

Mr. Johnson said, "I wish Swenson had some competition, then maybe he would buy more wagons and keep his teamsters sober a little more. It's getting so you can't depend on'em anymore. You boys go on home. If they show up now, them teamsters can just load their own wagons."

Later that evening Grady was soaking in his new watering hole, which was quite a ways upstream from his original place for a bath. Every time he passed one of those Mexican women on the street they grinned at him and his face turned red.

He kept thinking about what Mr. Johnson said about the freight wagons. *I wonder how much money it would take to get a wagon and a team. I have been saving my money again. I have almost seventy dollars.*

This time he did not carry it in his pocket. He had a special hiding place in the barn and checked it every evening when he came in.

I'll bet old Mr. Bledsoe can tell me what a wagon and team would cost

He walked into the barn and saw Mr. Bledsoe sitting at his desk, "Mr. Bledsoe, I've got a question for you."

"Okay sonny, what-cha got?"

"How much would a team of mules and a freight wagon cost?"

"About $500.00."

"How much money could a fellow make if he had a good team and wagon?"

"About $50.00 a day after expenses. If the injunes don't steal his mules and burn his wagon."

"Did you say $50.00 a day?"

"Yep."

"That'd be $300.00 in one week?"

"Yep, if he had a load to haul ever day."

Grady left there and moseyed over to May's. Pondering how he could raise $500.00 quick. As he sat down Ronnie and Lonnie walked in. Then an idea hit him.

CHAPTER SIX

Back at the ranch. Colleen heard a knock on the door. When she opened it, Jud was standing there. "What're you doing out here at the ranch? What do you want?"

He grabbed her and kissed her on the mouth, and said, "Is that any way to greet your future husband?"

She jerked back and wiped the back of her hand across her lips. Then in one continuous motion back handed him across the face. "If you ever do that again, I'll get a gun and kill you."

He was stunned, then regained his composure. "You little hell-cat, I'll do a lot more than that before I'm through. Tell your old man I need to see him." He pushed in past her.

Her father heard someone talking and stepped out of the back bedroom. He looked at Colleen and could tell by the look on her face she was upset. "What're you doing out here Jud?"

Jud had a bright red mark on the left side of his face. He said, "You need to tell this little hell-cat daughter of yours she'd better start being a lot nicer to me. You could get shot and then she would need a man around for sure."

Colleen thought, *Is he threatening my father? Dad used to be as quick as anybody with a gun, but with his arthritis he wouldn't have a chance.*

"Colleen, get your dad and me some coffee. We need to sit down and calmly have us a talk."

Her dad saw the look on her face and walked over to the stove and picked up the coffee pot with his right hand and with his left, grabbed two cups. "Sit down Jud and tell me what brings you out to the ranch."

Jud noticed what had happened and looked at Colleen with a smirk.

"Look, I don't want to be heartless. I'm very fond of Colleen and I want to marry her. It ain't right for us to have squabbling in the family. Now Colleen honey you need to come over here and sit down. We all need to talk."

Colleen stared at him but didn't move from where she stood.

"Look I know you've got a younger daughter back east in school. The bank loaned you money so you could pay her tuition. Colleen, if we get married, I'll see that baby sister is taken care of. Call it a business deal, if you want. I get a beautiful wife, and your daddy gets to keep half interest in the ranch. You'll be well taken care of. You'll make a beautiful hostess when we entertain important people. The railroad will eventually come." *A lot quicker than you know.* "This area will be filling up with new people, you and I'll be two of the most influential people in the state. I hope to become the governor of the state of Texas in a few years and you'll be the first lady. Colleen, you know I'm very fond of you but I also need you."

Colleen looked at her father and thought of her little sister. The one they had sent back east to get an education. She had one more year before she would be finished with school. What will happen to her if we lose the ranch? Then she looked at Jud and her stomach felt sick. *Am I being selfish? Just because I hate that arrogant selfish jackass, do I have the right to say no and let Dad lose the ranch and Marlene be forced out of school?*

Before she could say anything Jud went on, "Here's my deal. Old man I'll give you $500.00 and rip up your note. You will sign over half interest in the ranch to me and I'll become the managing partner. Colleen and I'll be married and I'll build us a nice big house suitable for entertaining important guests. You can continue to live here. I'll send the school tuition for next year so baby sister won't have to worry about getting kicked out of school? Do we have a deal?"

"What's the $500.00 for?" Colleen asked.

"So my father-in-law can have walking around money."

"Dad, he wants to buy your daughter and steal your ranch at the same time."

"Jud, you're wearing a gun. Let me reach over there and strap mine on and then let's walk out in the yard and settle this right now just you and me."

⇒⊹ ⊹⇐

Grady was sitting in the café when Ronne and Lonnie came in.

"Hey Grady, can we come and sit with you?"

"Yeah, in fact I've got an idea I want to discuss with you guys." Grady saw that the doctor had loosened the wires on Ronnie's teeth some and he could open his mouth a little so he wasn't having to drink all his food through the rubber tube.

"You guys got any money?"

"Sure Grady, we got eight or nine dollar a piece. We can pay for our own breakfast."

"Oh I know that but I mean any real money. Like $200.00 or $300.00 a piece."

"Lord no, we ain't never seen that much, the most we ever saw was,"---and then he realized what he was about to say and stopped in mid-sentence.

Grady laughed, "You almost said the most you ever saw was when you whacked me on the head with a chunk of stove wood. That's okay. That's all behind us now. I've got an idea that'll makes us all $200.00 or $300.00 a piece."

"Grady, are you planning on robbing the bank?"

"No. Lonnie, I figure you're a pretty good fighter, you just got your chin cracked before you knew what was coming. Ronnie you were a real good fighter, I just got a lucky punch and caught you with your jaw hanging open. Otherwise you might have whupped me. Here's the deal."

"I'll go around town and set up a fight between me and Lonnie. We'll put up a ring and charge people $1.00 to come and watch us fight. They'll pay it because they'll think you're still mad at me for breaking Ronnie's jaw."

"Grady, we ain't still mad at you. It was a fair fight."

"I know that, but a lot of people don't. So here's what we'll do. We'll pretend to be real mad at each other. People will see us arguing out in the street. We'll get the marshal to agree to be the referee. We'll do everything by Cornish rules."

"What does that mean?"

"We'll fight twelve rounds, each round ends when one of us gets knocked down. When a round ends we'll go back to our corner of the ring and sit down for one minute then the marshal will call us back to the center of the ring and we'll fight until another one gets knocked down. At the end of twelve rounds, the marshal will pick the winner unless one of us gets knocked out before then."

"Grady, you ain't gonna break my jaw too are ya?"

"No, just don't be fighting with your mouth open."

"How much money do ya think we can make?"

"Now Lonnie this ain't going to be no pretend fight. We're going to give the people their money's worth. You may whip me. That's okay if you do, you do, because no matter who wins we get the money. I get half for setting it up and everything, you guys split the other half. Deal?"

"Do you really think we could make $300 or $400 dollars?'

"That's off the ticket sales. Here's how we're going to make the big money."

CHAPTER SEVEN

olleen spoke up and said, "No Daddy, even if you won. That note would still be unpaid and somebody else would claim it. Jud your proposal is evil on its face. It is also practical. Give me a couple of weeks to get used to the idea."

"I've got business to attend to, I can't wait any longer. I'll give you until the first of the month and then we'll get married and close the deal. I figure you and I will go to San Francisco for a honeymoon then when we get back I'll start building us a grand house."

The thought of honeymooning with Jud made her want to throw up. She said, "Give me till the first."

She thought, *Lord, if you are going to do anything to help me out of this I need you to do it before the first of the month.*

After Jud left there was another knock on the door, it was a kid delivering a telegram. It was from Marlene:

Coming home for a visit---stop--- School shut down for a summer break--- riding train to Dallas---stop---stage to Abilene ---stop--- be there next week.

Colleen said, "Oh, my-gosh. Daddy, Marlene's coming home."

"When? Why's she coming home? She's paid up through this year."

"The school's closed for summer break."

"When's she going to get here?"

"Next week."

In her excitement she temporarily forgot the horror that was facing her in two weeks. She never noticed that her sister was riding the train all the way to Dallas.

The next morning Grady walked into the mill and Lonnie said, "You broke my brother's jaw. I'm not going to let you get away with that you know. He can't fight. But by thunder I can."

"It was a fair fight, leave me alone."

Mr. Johnson looked up and thought *where did that come from? Last week they were all buddy -buddy.*

Grady walked into May's for supper as Ronnie and Lonnie were coming out. Ronnie said, "You think you're a tough guy just because you got lucky one time." They stormed on past him out the door.

When he sat down May said, "You better watch yourself. Those two appear to be still mad."

"I ain't afraid of a bunch of talk."

The next morning all three of the boys walked into Mr. Johnson's office. He looked up and said, "What's this all about?"

"Mr. Johnson, do you remember when you said you wished you had some more freight wagons?"

"Well, me and the boys want to start our own freight company."

"Where do you plan to get the money to buy freight wagons and mules?"

"We want to set up a prize fight, Cornish rules between me and Lonnie. We'll charge $1.00 a head to watch it. We want you to help

Ronnie sell the tickets and collect the money. We thought we'd get the marshal to be the referee."

"So that's what all this jawin' has been about. You rascals. I wondered what happened. Last week ya'll was buddies and this week you fussin' all the time."

Grady grinned, "I figured if people thought we was really mad, a lot more folks would pay their dollar."

"So you're not only the fighter, you're also the promoter. Where do you plan to stage this fight?"

"We thought we could get some ropes and stretch them around four posts we sunk in the area out behind the hotel and people could sit on the hotel balcony to see it. If they can't get close enough."

"Do I get paid anything for going along with this nonsense?"

"We figured we'd give you five cents out of every dollar we take in."

"You two know one of you can get hurt don't cha? Just look at Ronnie. I ain't going to go along with this if it ain't gonna be a real fight."

Lonnie said, "Oh, it's gonna be a real fight. Grady hit me with a sucker punch last time."

"I thought you three were friends now."

"Oh we are, this is business now," Grady said.

"Have you talked to the marshal? Is he gonna go along with this?"

"No sir we'd like to go over and talk to him now if it's alright."

Mr. Johnson said "Go ahead I'm curious to see what he has to say."

The three walked over to the marshal's office.

"What're you three up to?"

"Marshal we want to have a prize fight. Cornish style"

"Who'll be fightin'?

"Me and Lonnie."

"When do you want to put on this fight?"

"Saturday after next. We'd like for you to be the referee."

He raised his eyebrows, "If I agree to do this, it's going to be by the rules. It's gonna be a clean fight and a real fight. Cause if you're trying to pull a scam I'll throw all three of ya in jail and keep you there until the circuit judge comes back around and I'll see to it that he won't be back around very soon."

"No sir that's why we want you to be the referee, so everybody can see it's a real fight. We plan on selling tickets for $1.00 to watch the fight and Mr. Johnson has agreed to be the cashier."

The marshal chuckled and said, "I'll bet that old scalawag is taking a percentage ain't he?"

"Yes sir we're going to give him a nickel out of every dollar."

"Then I want the same thing Johnson is gonna get. Where do you plan to put on this fight?"

"We figure we can put four posts in the ground out behind the hotel and stretch some ropes around them. That way people can sit on the balcony of the hotel if they can't get close enough to see."

"I'll give you boys' credit that's pretty smart. If people hear about it they'll probably come from miles around to watch two knuckle heads go at it. Don't either one of you get hurt between now and then."

Ronnie and Lonnie went back to the feed mill and Grady went down to the newspaper office. When he walked in a man with an ink stained apron said, "Yes sir, what can I do for you?"

"I've got a story for your paper."

"Oh yeah, what kind of story?"

"There's going to be a prize fight here in town. Cornish rules style."

The man with the apron looked with more interest, "Who's going to be fighting?"

"Me and Lonnie Higgins."

"Is that the brother of the guy who got his jaw busted in a fight?"

"Yes sir."

"Are you the one who busted that fellow's jaw?"

"Yes sir."

He looked at Grady, then said, "He'll have you by thirty pounds and his arms are longer than yours. What makes you think you can beat him?"

Grady grinned and said, "I whupped both of'em at the same time last time so I guess I can handle one this time."

The man picked up a pencil and started writing. "When's this fight gonna take place?"

"Saturday after next."

"Are you gonna sell tickets to watch you two fight?"

"Yes sir tickets will be one dollar. The marshal has agreed to be the referee. The fight'll be Cornish rules, for twelve rounds. If we are both standing at the end of twelve rounds the marshal will declare the winner."

"Do you really think you can last twelve rounds?"

"No sir, I don't reckon I'll have to."

With the fight set Grady and Knot went to the wagon yard. As he walked in a man sitting before a roll top desk asked, "What can I do for ya?"

"I need to buy a freight wagon. I think I'd prefer a T.G.Mandt wagon."

"I don't have any in the yard, I do have a Stoughton wagon coming in, should be here next Sunday. You know it's the same wagon. After old man Mandt pulled out, the company kept making the same wagons under a different name. Cost you $400.00. Have you got a good set of mules?"

"Not yet."

"I know a widow lady that's got a good set of draft mules. Her husband died last fall when he got bit by a rattlesnake. She needs the money so she'll sell'em."

"I'd like to buy the wagon, but I don't have the money yet."

"Son, I can't hold it for ya, I've got a rancher supposed to come in next few days that's why I ordered it."

"If I give you $40.00 will you hold it till Monday for me?"

"If you ain't got the money what makes you think you're gonna have it?"

Grady told him about the fight, "You see I get half the money, whether I win or lose."

"This other feller, is he as big as you?"

"He outweighs me about thirty pounds and he's about four inches taller than me. You know those twin brothers, the Higgins boys?"

"Wait a minute are you the feller that busted ole Ronnie's jaw?"

"Yep, and now I'll be fightin' the other one, Lonnie."

"Well, hell I'd give a dollar to see that myself. Okay you give me $40.00 and I'll hold the freighter until Tuesday. If you don't show up you'll lose your $40.00 'cause there ain't no refunds."

Grady gave him the money and they shook hands on the deal. Grady looked down and said, "Come on Knot we got ourselves a wagon."

CHAPTER EIGHT

Two days later, Jud walked into the saloon, the two railroad men were sitting at a table over in the corner. "Gentlemen you are invited to my wedding Saturday after next. Then we will close the deal for the right-of-way through the gap as soon as you pay me the $5,000.00."

"Jud be reasonable. You know the railroad ain't never paid that kind-a money for a right-of-way."

"I'll tell you what I do know."

"It's gonna cost you a lot more than $5,000.00 if you have to reroute that entire section any other way."

"We are not authorized to pay that much money. We'll have to send a wire back to headquarters and see what they say."

"Well either way I'll be getting married to the prettiest redhead in the territory a week from Saturday. I'll be the managing partner of one of the biggest ranches in the area. Let me know what head-quarters has to say." He stood up and walked out the door.

A newspaper boy was selling papers on the board walk. "READ ALL ABOUT IT, PRIZE FIGHT COMING TO TOWN.

Jud struck a match and lit up a cigar. Then reached in his pocket and gave the boy a nickel.

He flipped open the paper and the headlines read:

PRIZE FIGHT COMING TO ABILENE

A sporting event between two local men is scheduled a week from Saturday at 10:00 in the morning. September 3rd in the year of our Lord 1879. An arena will be erected in the vacant lot behind the hotel. Tickets will sell for $1.00 each.

The two fighters are Lonnie Higgins of Abilene and Grady McCain an orphaned boy from the Boys Home who now works for the feed mill.

Pastor Sullivan has agreed to say a prayer for both the fighters before the contest begins. Marshal Taylor has agreed to referee the fight and assure that its run by the Cornish fighting rules. The fight will be for twelve rounds. The contestants will fight until one man gets knocked down. That will signal an end to that round. Each fighter will go back to his corner for a one minute rest, then the marshal will call them back to the center of the ring and a new round will begin.

If a fighter is knocked out the fight is over and the one standing will be the winner

If a fighter is unable to toe the mark to start the next round he will be disqualified and the one toeing the mark will be declared the winner.

When asked if he thought he stood a chance of winning the fight Grady said "I whipped both of those Higgins boys at the same time once. I reckon I can whip one now."

When asked for his response to Grady's statement Lonnie said, "He caught me when I had a hundred pound sack of feed in my hands and hit me with a sucker punch.

I ain't gonna have no hundred pound sack of feed in my hands this time."

It should be a good contest. Both fighters are in good shape they have been loading one hundred pound bags of feed over at the feed mill.

Jud thought, *here is a chance to make some real money. I'll bet that Higgins boy will whop the tar out of the orphaned boy.*

Colleen came back from the mercantile and found her father slumped over the settee. She said, "Daddy, are you okay?"

He didn't answer, she looked closer at him and ran out the door and grabbed the first horse she saw. Raced all the way to the doctor's house. "Doctor Baker, Come quick something's wrong with my dad."

Doctor Baker grabbed his black bag and the two of them ran out the door. He jumped into his buggy and dashed to the O'Shanity house. The doctor took his stethoscope and listened to Mr. O'Shanity heart. Then said, "Colleen, honey you are going to have to help me get him into bed."

A few minutes later the doctor said, "Colleen has he been under a lot of stress lately?"

She hesitated a moment and then said, "He had a note over at the bank. As you know we could not make a cattle drive last year because it was too dry. Jud showed up here saying he had bought the note from the bank and demanding that daddy pay it. Or else he was going to take the ranch."

"Colleen, how much is the note for?"

"It's only $700.00."

"He's threatening to take the whole ranch for only $700.00. How many head of cattle does your daddy have out there?"

"Over 2,000 head."

They are bringing about $15.00 a head if you only sold a thousand they would bring about $15,000.00. This just ain't right. Honey if I had $700.00 I'd loan it to you right now so you could pay that low down sniveling varmint off. But I don't have any walking around money."

"After hearing that story now I understand. That explains it. Colleen it looks like you daddy has had a stroke. That kind of stress for a proud man like your daddy could bring on a stroke."

"What can you do?"

"There ain't much I can do. We'll just have to keep him still and quiet for a few days and see if he comes out of it. Sometimes they come back with little or no side effect. Sometimes they are paralyzed on one side or the other. We won't know for a few days. I'm sorry." He patted her on the shoulder and said, "I'll be back in a couple of hours to check on him if anything changes run back over and get me."

Colleen didn't know what else to do so she sat down and opened up the family Bible. It fell open to the ninth chapter of Psalms and her eyes fell to the ninth verse. **Psalms 9:9 read, *The LORD is a stronghold for the oppressed, a stronghold in times of trouble.***

Colleen thought, *Lord there can't be anybody more oppressed right now than me. My daddy may be dying or paralyzed, an evil man is forcing me to marry him. What can I do? If I just had $700.00 I could pay off that note and make that horror go away. Lord I need a miracle. I need two miracles. I need for you to make my daddy well again and I need Jud to go away. Lord, why couldn't it have been Jud who had a stroke?* Then she said *"Lord I am sorry I thought that, I know you did say pray for your enemies but right now it's hard. Please help me. Amen?"*

CHAPTER NINE

Monday morning of the second week Grady woke with a fever. He ached all over. His stomach felt queasy. He felt like he was dying of thirst. Crawling out of the hayloft he stumbled to the well pump and worked the handle until cool refreshing water gushed out. After he drank his fill he bathed his head, chest and shoulders and felt a little bit better.

He started to May's for breakfast but as soon as he smelled the bacon frying he dashed between two buildings and started up-chucking.

I better go see doc, this is not good, I need to get to work, plus I've got a fight in six days.

Grady stumbled into Doctor Baker's office. Doctor Baker looked up when Grady came in, "What's the matter Grady?"

"I don't know doc, I feel terrible. You need to give me something so I can go to work."

"Climb up on the examining table so I can take a look at you."

The first thing the doc did was stick a thermometer in Grady's mouth. Then proceed to ask him questions. "Have you been coughing?"

"Yah-a-little."

"Have you been throwing up?"

"Nnnnnnnoough." He jerked the thermometer out of his mouth and said, "Dang it, doc I can't answer your questions with this thing sticking in my mouth."

"Stick it back in there or I got another one I'll stick up your rear end. I heard what you said, did you hear what I just said?"

Grady jammed that thermometer back in his mouth, quick.

The doc looked in his ears pushed on his stomach and prodded all over, then took the thermometer out of his mouth. "Humm, it looks like you have a fever. Your temperature is 101. Let me hear you cough."

"I'd say you've got bronchitis. I'm going to give you some medicine, but you don't need to go to work for a few days."

"Doc, Lonnie and me have got a fight in five days."

"You're not going to have a fight in five days. You'll have to post-pone that fight."

There is no way we can post-pone the fight. It is already the talk of the town. Ronnie is already holding a lot of bets, on it. It is funny how the betting is about fifty-fifty on me and on Lonnie. Plus that man will only hold the wagon till Tuesday. It would probably take weeks for him to get another one from the factory. If we disappoint the people by calling it off, we may not get a crowd next time.

Tuesday morning Grady's head felt like a base drum. Every time he took a deep breath he got into a coughing fit, and couldn't get his breath for several seconds. He finally crawled down from the loft and stumbled over to May's for breakfast.

He forced down two eggs and some bacon, washed it down with three cups of cowboy coffee. Crawled back up into the hayloft and slept. He woke in the middle of the afternoon soaking wet with sweat. *Maybe that's a good sign. Maybe the fever has broken.* He had a raging thirst. Climbing down from the loft he saw Mr. Johnson and Bledsoe talking by the door to the barn.

Mr. Johnson said, "I don't think there's any way in the world Grady's gonna be ready to fight Lonnie by Saturday. He can't even come to work."

"Boy I'm gonna be in trouble if he can't cause I bet everything I've got on him." Bledsoe said.

"Me too because I watched how he handled those two the first time. I bet nearly everything I've got on him too."

The two men walked away so he couldn't hear what they said after that.

Grady sat down on a bale of hay and scratched Knot's ears. "Wow. That's bad, I've got to get my strength back. I can't let them lose all they've got bet on me."

Wednesday morning Marleen stepped off the train in Dallas and walked to the telegraph window at the train station. The man with the green sun shade said, "Yes ma'am, what can I do for a pretty lady like you?"

"I would like to send a telegram to Abilene please."

He handed her a pad of printed telegram forms and a pencil. "Sweetie they make me charge by the word. So make is short and simple."

She wrote:

Arrived Dallas-stop-leaving on noon stage-stop- be there time for supper tomorrow- Stop- Marlene

"That is thirteen words so I'll have to charge you sixty-five-cents."

Marlene counted out the coins and walked to the café across the street from the train station. A handsome young man in a business suit offered to carry her bag across the street. She said, "That is very nice of you sir. The bag is not heavy, I appreciate your kindness but I will carry it myself."

He tipped his hat and scurried away.

Marlene thought, *I have been back east too long. I forgot what Texas gentlemen are like. The next good looking guy who offers to carry my bag, I might just let him--- especially if he's a cowboy.*

⤙ ⤚

Jud was holding shop in the saloon. "Okay boys I'm giving three to one odds on Grady McCain beating Lonnie Higgins in the fight this weekend. Anybody want to triple your money?"

"I heard he's been sick."

"Now boys you know that's an old trick in the fight game. One of the contestants pretends to be sick before the fight to get more people to bet on his opponent. Then he shows up fit as a fiddle and wins all the money. Hey if you bet it's a gamble. I'm giving three to one odds if you want to play step up and put your bets down."

Ronnie and Lonnie had already collected over $100.00 in ticket sales, Lonnie said, "You don't suppose ole Grady is faking it do ya?"

"Nah, he looked pretty sick when I saw him."

"You know we fought him and he's a pretty good fighter. We've got over $100.00, if we bet it and Grady did win we'd get back $300.00. That'd give us $100.00 a piece even if we didn't sell any more tickets."

"Ronnie you gotta make the bet. Cause it might not look right if I bet against myself you know."

CHAPTER TEN

Thursday morning, Grady got his chores done early and walked over to May's. May saw him when he walked in the door. She went back in the kitchen and whipped up a concoction in a tall glass and brought it to him. "Are you still going to get in that fight Saturday?"

"I reckon so it seems a lot of folks are bettin' on me and I'd hate to see them lose by default."

"Here drink all of this down. It'll help you get your strength back."

"What is it?"

"Grady don't ask no questions just drink it down. It'll help you get your strength back. Trust me. "

Grady took it and drank it down, it didn't tastes bad. In fact it was pretty good.

May watched him then said, "Now get a good breakfast in ya. Today and tomorrow come in at lunch and drink another one of those. I'm gonna fix you one three times a day for the next two days. Just don't say nothin' to nobody about it. I've got a $50.00 bet on you so I'm gonna help you all I can."

"You bet $50.00 on me?"

"Yeah, so hush and eat your breakfast."

Lonnie and Ronnie walked into the café and when they saw Grady pulled up a chair across from him.

Ronnie said, "Grady, have you really been sick? You ain't fakin' it are ya?"

"No, why would you say that?"

"Jud is telling everybody in town that you're just fakin' being sick to get more people to bet their money on Lonnie. So he's giving three to one odds to get some people to bet on you."

Grady said, "Oh my goodness that's why May bet $50.00 on me."

"Well I did too," Ronnie said.

"What? Where did you get any money to bet?"

"From all the tickets we sold already." They were both grinning like they had pulled off something.

"Are you two crazy? Who placed the bet? That's the craziest thing I ever heard of. Now if I were to win it'll look like you threw the fight."

Lonnie said, "Oh, I didn't bet anything. Ronnie's the one who placed the bet."

Now Grady was getting mad his voice raised, "You're the stupidest two I have ever met."

Other people in the cafe turned to look at them.

Lonnie jumped up and said, "Don't you call me and my brother stupid. We'll see Saturday who's the stupid one."

Jud walked in at that time and thought, *yes that'll get a few more bets down.*

CHAPTER ELEVEN

With a loud crack of a whip and a loud rebel yell the stage thundered into town. A cloud of dust rolled over it when it stopped. Marleen lifted her skirt over her dainty slim ankles and stepped down. The driver handed her bag down to her. As she reached for it a handsome man reached past her and took the bag.

"You must be Marleen."

"I'm sorry sir, I don't think I know you."

Holding her bag in his left hand he removed his hat with his right, "Please allow me to introduce myself, I'm Jud Rawlins at your service. Your sister Colleen told me she had a sister coming soon. She never told me how beautiful you would be."

"You know my sister?"

"Yes, I know Colleen and your father."

"I'm expecting them to meet me. I sent a cable telling them I'd be on this stage. Where's my father and Colleen? Why did they send you?"

"I'm afraid I have some bad news. They're over at the doctor's home. Your father is quiet ill. Come I'll take you there." He took her arm.

As they walked toward the doctors house Jud said the strangest thing, he said, "Marleen, you are quiet beautiful. You would make a great wife for the governor of Texas."

When Jud and Marleen walked into the doctor's house Colleen looked up and was horrified by what she saw. She saw Jud holding on to her baby sister's arm with one hand and carrying her bag with the other. He was staring at her like a mountain lion looking at a new born calf.

"Marleen when did you get here?"

"I was on the stage. Didn't you get my wire?"

"Oh yes, I did, I've been so worried about father, I didn't realize what time it was. I'm so sorry."

"That's okay, thanks for sending Jud to meet me."

"I didn't send....Jud what're you doing here?"

"Colleen, why didn't you tell me your sister was a raving beauty?"

"Get your hand off of her. If you ever touch her again I'll get father's gun and shoot you. I mean it. Get out of this house right now."

"Colleen, what has gotten into you? Jud has been a perfect gentleman."

CHAPTER TWELVE

Jud walked into the saloon later that evening and saw Ronnie and Lonnie having a beer. "I heard that Grady called you brothers stupid in front of a bunch of people this morning. Is that right?"

"Yes he did."

"Well when you whip his tail Saturday and walk away with all those winnings at three to one odds, Lonnie, who'll look like the stupid one then?"

Ronnie said, "Don't forget Lonnie we only get half of all the money. We've got to give him the other half."

"Why does he get fifty percent and you only twenty-five each." Jud asked.

"That was the deal. He would get up the fight, and he would get half of the money we collect from selling the tickets and we would split the other half." Ronnie answered.

"Why does he get two quarters and each of you only get one quarter. Isn't Lonnie going to be fighting just as hard as he is?"

"Yeah but that's what he said. He said, I'll fight with Lonnie and I'll get half of the money and you two can split the other half."

"Well that is just off the ticket sales. If you win a bunch of money he doesn't get any of the winnings. At least to me he shouldn't. You did that on your own didn't you?"

"Yeah, in fact he got real mad and called us stupid when he found out we done it."

"Well seems to me that proves he ain't got no claim on the winnings. Have you got any more you want to put up and really show him you're not stupid when you walk away with all of that money Saturday?"

Grady said, "Come on Knot let's go for a run. I need to build up my wind a little bit before Saturday. Knot, I still can't believe those idiots went and bet the money we collected with Jud. We could end up with nothing if I don't win."

The dog cocked its head to one side and looked at him.

They jogged on for another mile then doubled back to the barn.

Marleen walked into the bedroom and looked down at their father. He looked so pale and lifeless. "Colleen, is he going to be alright? Is he going to get better?"

"Marlene, we don't know. The doctor said one of three things will happen and we don't know which one it will be right now. He could get better and have no side effects from the stroke. He could be paralyzed. He could die. The doctor said, 'It's up to God, there's nothing we can do.' All we can do is watch and pray. Believe me I've been praying?"

"Colleen, why were you so rude to Jud last night, he is very handsome and he was such a gentleman. I've never seen you act so rude to anyone."

"Marleen, sit down I've got some things I need to tell you. You've been gone for two years. Last year we had the worst drought this state has ever seen. Daddy could not make a cattle drive to market. If a ranch doesn't sell any steers they don't make any money. Daddy went over to the bank and borrowed $700.00 to buy a few supplies we needed and to pay your school tuition. Then a few weeks ago this stranger named Jud showed up and said he had bought the note from the bank and if daddy didn't pay it he was going to take the ranch because the bank had a lien on our ranch."

"Daddy will pay him when he makes a drive this year. "

"That's what daddy told Jud. He told him in a few weeks he would make a drive to market and come back and pay him. Jud said, "No, I want my money right now. You have got until next Monday to pay me or I will own the ranch."

"That's terrible," Marlene said.

"Oh it gets worse. He told daddy he would tear up the note and give daddy $500.00 cash, if I would marry him. He even grabbed me one time and kissed me right on the mouth."

"What did you do?"

"I slapped him so hard my hand hurt for two days."

"Good I'll bet that taught him some manners."

"No it did not. He came back the very next day and threatened Daddy. Daddy, even as old as he is, challenged him to a gun fight out in the front yard."

"Has daddy been shot?"

"No, daddy has had a stroke."

"What happened then?"

"I talked daddy out of getting into a gunfight with Jud by telling him if something happened to him you and I would be all alone."

"Colleen, Jud seemed so nice. I find this all hard to believe."

"Marleen look at your father. Jud is the reason he had a stroke. The doctor tells me strokes are brought on because of stress. Our father has been threatened with having his ranch stolen from him, his daughter violated, he has been threatened with being shot. Most of all he has been worried sick over what will happen to you and I if something happens to him and it has. That man that carried your bag for you is the same man that caused our father to be lying here on the verge of death. That is why I threated to get a gun and shoot him, if he didn't leave you alone and believe me I will. "

"I would never have let him touch my bag if I had known this."

"It's not your fault little sister, it's mine. If I had been there when the stage came in you would not have had to deal with him. If our father dies here is what I want us to do."

CHAPTER THIRTEEN

Grady set four posts exactly twenty feet apart and then got Ronnie to help him stretch two ropes tightly around the posts forming the ring. Some of the guys in town were erecting crude bleachers on two sides of the ring. There was so much excitement in town it felt like the circus was coming.

Today was only Thursday and already people were camping outside of town.

Jud was in his room at the hotel counting the money. He was holding over $10,000.00 and at three to one odds he was getting a lot of takers on Grady. So many now he was starting to get worried. What if by some miracle he won? Jud could never cover the bets. Maybe his best bet was to grab all of the money and sneak out of town. He could go to San Francisco or New York and live like a king for a while.

Then he thought, this is nothing, by fight time Saturday morning I could have thirty or forty thousand and when Grady loses I can keep it all. Then he started thinking about ways to guarantee that Grady could not win.

If the fight went all twelve rounds, he could offer to split some with the marshal if he declared Lonnie the winner. The old fuddy duddy would probably turn him down and throw him in jail for suggesting it.

The man has been sick so he probably will not last twelve rounds. He'll be too weak, not enough strength to go twelve rounds. Between each round he has to come back to his corner and sit down for one minute. I've got a plan that will make sure he doesn't toe the mark for round twelve if he gets that far.

⟫⟪ ⟫⟪

Grady had finished tightening the ropes and was walking back to the livery when he saw Colleen walk out of the mercantile in from of him, he said, "Hello Colleen. How's your father today?"

He was speechless, when a redhead even more beautiful than Colleen turned around. It wasn't Colleen.

"I'm sorry I don't know you. Do you know my sister?"

His tongue wouldn't work, he couldn't make words. All he could do was stare and turn red in the face.

She smiled the most dazzling smile Grady had ever seen, and said, "How do you know Colleen?"

Grady whipped off his hat and stuttered, "Ch ch cH Church."

"How nice of you to ask about my father. He is no different yet. We are still praying for his recovery. My name is Marleen, I am the younger sister. I have been away at school. I didn't catch your name."

"Grady McCain. I work at the feed mill."

"Well Mr. McCain. I'll tell Colleen you inquired about father. Good day."

Grady just stood there with his hat in his hands staring glassy eyed after her.

Knot nudged him with his nose. "Oh Lord Knot, I didn't know a woman could be that beautiful. I've gotta win that fight so she'll notice me. So I'll have some money."

"Colleen I just met a handsome young friend of yours."

"Who would that be?"

"Probably the most handsome cowboy in all of Texas. His name is Grady McCain. How come you never told me about him?"

"I don't know a Grady McCain."

"Well he certainly knows you. When I walked out of the mercantile a good looking cowboy walked up behind me and said, 'Colleen how is your father?' "

"He said he knew you at church. Well he sort of said that. I asked him where he knew my sister and he stuttered out the word church."

"I still don't remember him. What does he look like?"

"A Greek God in a cowboy hat."

"Oh wait a minute he has reddish hair and he is about your age."

"Yes."

"I have seen him around town. We have never actually been introduced, that I remember. He works over at the feed mill. The way I heard it two bullies jumped on him and he whipped 'em both. One had to eat his meals through a rubber tube for a few days after the fight. Everybody in town is talking about a big fight that is going to be fought Saturday between that boy and one of the big bullies."

"So he is a prize fighter?" Marlene said.

"No, the thing I have heard was that his parents were killed, and he grew up out at the boys ranch. When he turned eighteen he left the boys ranch and got a job at the feed mill. These two brothers have been picking on all the young men and boys that are smaller than them. This one didn't back down from them."

"Are you going to watch the fight?" Marleen asked.

"The pastor has a space reserved on one of the balconies, he has invited us to join them. I think it would be exciting to watch."

"Yes, but I don't want to see Grady get hurt."

"Marlene, it will help to get our mind off worrying about father for a few minutes. Another thing is I bet some money on Grady, so

I hope he wins. If he wins I can pay off that note and stop worrying about losing the ranch."

"What if he loses? You aren't seriously thinking about marrying that Jud are you?"

"Marlene, I've been reading my Bible and praying. Maybe God is gonna have Grady win so I won't have to worry about it anymore."

CHAPTER FOURTEEN

Friday morning dawned bright and clear. As far as Grady could see there was not one cloud in the sky. The morning sky was a beautiful shade of blue.

"Come on Knot, let's go for a run. I still need to get my wind back."

As he ran he thought I feel a little stronger. *I finally found out what's in that concoction May has been making me drink. She mixes raw eggs in milk with cinnamon, vanilla and honey. It actually taste pretty good. She said it would build back stamina fast. I sure hope she's right.*

When he went into May's for breakfast he felt like every person in the café was watching him. Without asking him what he wanted May brought him four eggs and a thick slab of steak. "Eat all of that, you need it."

One of the deputy marshals came over to his table, "Grady do you have a second in your corner tomorrow? I'm Jacob Swenson, I boxed in the old country. I will be happy to be your second if you want me too."

Grady stuck out his hand and shook Swenson's hand. "I appreciate any help I can get. Have a seat." When the man sat down Grady asked, "You said the old country. Where would that be?"

"Sweden. I was on the national bare knuckle boxing team. I am pretty good at fixing cuts in a hurry."

"That's good because I may need a few fixed tomorrow. Man I wish I had known you a few weeks ago, maybe you could teach me some things. No time now."

"Have you done any boxing before?"

"I grew up out at the boys ranch and Father O'Malley was a real fan of the sport of boxing. We held matches every three months. He had boxed at Oxford before he went to seminary. He was a pretty good coach I guess. Of course I never saw anybody box except the boys he trained."

"I will be watching each round so I will try to give you tips between rounds. That is the best I can do on this short notice. The fight starts tomorrow at 10:00. Eat a hearty supper but don't eat any breakfast. A man moves faster on an empty stomach, and he can take punches in the belly better."

"Does the other fighter need a second?"

"I guess his brother will be his second."

"Has he ever boxed?"

"I doubt if either of them have ever been in a ring. They have done plenty of rough and tumble fighting though."

"Don't sell him short Grady, that kind of fighter can be tough. However, skill almost always wins over brawn. I want you to take it easy today. Conserve any energy you have stored up. Drink plenty of water today but no water in the morning before the bout begins. I will meet you here in the morning and we will get ready. We might not win but we will make a fight out of it that is for sure."

Jud strutted around smoking a big cigar. Acting like he was already the governor of Texas. When he walked into the cafe, Colleen and Marleen were sitting at a table. Jud walked directly to their table, removed his hat and bowed to Marleen. "Today my dear you look more beautiful than before. Would you be so gracious as to allow me the pleasure of joining you for coffee?"

Before Marleen could answer Colleen said, "Sir we are discussing private family business. We do not care to share it with anyone else. So if you will excuse us. We would rather be alone."

Jud shot her a look that would sour milk and said, "Marleen, you are over eighteen do you still allow your big older sister to make decisions for you?"

"No sir, I make my own decisions, but in this case I agree with Colleen. So please excuse us."

He bowed to Marleen and said, "I shall see you again my fair lady." Picked up her right hand and kissed it, then walked away.

Marleen said, "He is a scoundrel but you'll have to admit he is handsome and gallant."

"So is a copperhead snake but he will still bite you and make you die. Marleen don't be deceived by pretty things that are out to harm you. That is the man who for all practical purposes killed our father, and is trying to steal our ranch. Which is our home."

"Oh Colleen, I know you're right, but that was the first time a man ever kissed my hand. It was thrilling. Colleen what are we going to do if Grady doesn't win the fight tomorrow?"

"I don't know. If he does win I am going to get the marshal to escort me over to Jud's place and pay off the note in front of witnesses and I hope I never see that man again."

"If Grady wins, he will have a lot of money. I wonder what he plans to do with it." Marleen mused.

Colleen said, "This is a small town, not much goes on that everybody else doesn't know about it. I hear that he has already paid a down payment on a freight wagon and is planning to start his own freight company. So if he wins he will pay off the wagon and go into the freight business. I hope he does real well. I am told he is honest and hard working. Lord knows we need another freight hauling company in this area the one we've got now stays drunk most of the time."

"Colleen, I wonder what the railroad would do to his freight hauling business. You know I rode the train all the way to Dallas. The conductor told me they would be all the way to Abilene within three weeks. He said if I stayed one week longer I could ride a train all the way to Boston."

CHAPTER FIFTEEN

The railroad man said, "Look Jud, stop stalling. Get reasonable, the track laying crew will be here with in the next three weeks. We need that right-of-way now."

"You get my $5,000.00. I'll have that right-of-way signed by Monday morning. Now if you'll excuse me I believe our business is finished for today. Me and this little dance hall gal have got some business to take care of, don't we sugar?"

The railroad man said, "I have a dang good notion to go look up old man O'Shanity myself and see what we can do. Why do we need that pompous jerk?"

Someone knocked on the door, Colleen looked at Marleen, "Are you expecting anyone?"

"No. Let me see who it is."

"Don't you dare open that door until I get fathers six–shooter." She was back in a minute and said, "Now open the door."

When Marleen opened the door two men in business suits were standing there. "Are you Miss O'Shanity?"

"I am one of them. What can I do for you?"

Taking off his derby he said, "My name is Harris Miliband and this is Cliff Dunston we work for the railroad. We'd like to speak to your father."

Colleen who had been standing back with her father's six-shooter in her hands, said, "Gentlemen. We are not trying to be impolite but we do not know you and we are two women here alone. So we will not invite you in. However if you want to speak to our father he is under the doctors care and at the moment he is at the doctors house in Abilene. Good night gentlemen."

A short time later the two railroad men knocked on the door at the doctor's house. "Yes, gentlemen what can I do for you?"

"Doctor we have been told you have a Mr. O'Shanity as a patient. We are from the railroad and we have rather urgent business to discuss with him. Can he have visitors?"

"If you had asked me yesterday I would have said no. Today he has made a marvelous recovery. Oh he's not fully recovered, but he's dramatically improved. You gentlemen step in and wait right here while I check and see if he feels up to talking with you."

He was back in a moment and said, "Mr. O'Shanity would like to talk with you. Please follow me."

Two hours later the railroad men were drinking a beer in the saloon, one of them said, "To think we've been waiting all of that time with this Jud dude and he didn't have any legal authority at all."

"I'm glad you suggested we go talk to Mr. O'Shanity. Tomorrow morning we'll have the right-of-way lease signed and we won't have to pay no $5,000.00. In fact we could have gotten it for $500.00 but when I found out all it took to pay off his note, I have no problem offering him $1,000.00."

"We'll meet him at nine o'clock in the morning, sign the lease and give him a bank draft and still have time to watch the big fight."

Unknown to the two railroad men, Jud was sitting in a crib with one of the gals on the other side of a thin wall listening to every word they said.

⊨┼ ┼⊨

In the middle of the night a shadowy figure dressed in black slowly slid open the window on the side of the doctor's house next to the bedroom Mr. O'Shanity was sleeping in. Mr. O'Shanity woke instantly when someone slammed a pillow down over his face covering his nose and mouth. He tried to struggle but he was paralyzed on his left side.

Doctor Baker came in to check on Mr. O'Shanity the next morning and was stunned. He had been doing so well last night. Then he noticed blood on the bed near his right hand. Looking closer he saw that two of his finger nails were ripped off. "What in the world?"

Then the doctor noticed that his bottom lip had been bitten through. Now the doctors alarm was sky rocketing. Looking around the room he saw a pillow tossed on the floor between the window and the bed. There was a large spot of blood on the pillow.

He stepped out of the room and went over to the Marshall's office. As he walked in the marshal glanced up and said, "Hey doc what brings you out so early in the morning?"

"Dan, you need to come over to my house quick. Mr. O'Shanity is dead and I suspect he has been murdered."

"Murdered? Why would you think that, didn't the man have a stroke a few days ago?"

"Yes he did, but the last couple of days he has been coming out of it. In fact he made a deal last night with the railroad to lease the right-of-way for the tracks to cross his land. He was supposed to sign it this morning."

"Did you hear them make the deal?"

"Yeah, he called me in to witness; them shaking hands on the deal."

When the two men walked into the room the marshal said, "Judging by those finger nails I'd say he tried to put up a fight."

"He was paralyzed on his left side so he couldn't fight the intruder off but it looks like he tried."

The marshal stood looking at the body then said, "Maybe I should be looking for somebody with scratches on his face."

"Maybe, but probably not, a person's skin wouldn't have torn lose those finger nails like that. They were probably torn lose when he scratched heavy clothing."

The marshal reached down and picked up the pillow and turned it over, "Look here, you can see the claw marks. He tore his nails trying to claw the pillow off his face."

"Marshal whoever did this was a big man."

CHAPTER SIXTEEN

Doctor Baker went over to the church and got the pastor to come wait with him for the girls to arrive.

When Colleen and Marleen got to the doctor's house he met them at the door and said, "Come in girls I need to talk to you."

Colleen looked at the pastor standing there. She said, "What's wrong?"

"I am afraid I have some very bad news."

Marleen started crying, "Did he die?"

"Girls come into the parlor and sit down." The doctor said gently.

The pastor said, "Yes your father's gone. We have been talking and my wife and I want you two to come stay with us until you can figure out what you are going to do next."

Colleen bravely said, "We've got a home. We will go home."

"We don't think it's safe for you to do that right now."

"Why."

The doctor spoke up and said, "Girls somebody climbed in through the bedroom window last night and murdered your father."

Both girls said, "Murdered?"

"Yes."

"Who would do something like that? He had no enemies, he never hurt anybody in his life."

Marleen was sobbing uncontrollably.

Colleen wiped her eyes and said, "How did they kill him?"

"Someone held him down with a pillow over his face until he died."

"Are you saying some sneaking, sniveling coward climbed in the window of a paralyzed man's room and held a pillow over his face until he died? A man who couldn't defend himself?"

"What kind of low life coward would do something like that?' Then she said, "Jud. The last time he was out at our house Daddy told him to wait until he got his gun on and they would walk out in the yard and settle this right now and Jud left. He's the sneaking coward that did this. I'll get daddy's gun and kill him."

The pastor said, "Colleen, I know how you feel but the marshal has called in the county sheriff to help him find out for sure who did this, we can't rush to judgement. Right now we have no proof. My wife and I want you two to stay at our house for a few days until the sheriff and the marshal have a chance to find out for sure who did this then we'll know it's safe for you to go home."

━━◈ ◈━━

Jud walked into to the telegraph office as soon as it opened and said, "I need to send a wire."

The wire was sent to a lawyer in Austin, Texas it read:

File deed of possession Hill Valley Ranch, Taylor County, Abilene, Texas -stop- repossess to pay past due note—file deed of possession immediately.

When he walked out he said, "Now we'll see."

Jud walked into the café and ordered a big hearty breakfast. Confident that he would have it all before this day was gone. He would pay off the few suckers that were smart enough to bet on Lonnie, and keep all of the money bet on Grady. He smiled when he thought *then I'll move into my new ranch house, maybe I'll keep both of those sisters and have me a harem.*

Jud looked over and watched Lonnie shoveling steak and eggs into his mouth.

CHAPTER SEVENTEEN

"Sheriff, let's put your four deputies on horseback at the corners of the vacant lot." The marshal said, "That way they can see over the crowd and move quickly if they see anything that's suspicious. There's enough money bet here to cause somebody to want to do something that might affect the outcome of the fight."

"Good thinking. Where're your men going to be?"

"I'm going to have two men right down beside the ring. I'm going to have two on top of the hotel with rifles. I would feel better if you were up on one of the balconies of the hotel. This thing has gotten a lot bigger than I ever dreamed. I'll be in the ring with the fighters and I'll have a man standing at a neutral corner with two double barrel shot guns, if need be he can jump into the ring with me."

The pastor said, "Come on girls. There is nothing we can do right now so let's go watch the contest. It will help get your mind off the horrible events of this day for a few minutes. After the contest, we'll get busy and make plans."

"Okay Grady it's time to go." Jacob said, "There's one heck of a crowd waiting out there. Whether you win or whether you lose, you're going to give them a show. I feel good about that."

"I hope so. Jacob, I appreciate you being in my corner and I appreciate all the help you have given me so far."

"Grady, let's go, they came a long way and paid their money let's give'em one to remember."

When they walked out of the livery stable Grady was shocked at the size of the crowd. He looked at the vacant lot behind the hotel there must have been a thousand people. Then he glanced up at the balconies of the hotel and it was packed with men and women. In the third balcony from the left he saw the sun radiate off two sets of beautiful red hair. *Oh I just hope I don't look like a fool in front of them. If Lonnie knocks me out in the first round I hope it kills me. I'd rather die than face them after that.*

The crowd parted as Jacob and Grady came through. The marshal was already in the ring. Then he saw the crowd parting for Lonnie and Ronnie as they approached from the other side.

My God he looks bigger than I remember.

The marshal held up his hand for silence. When he had the crowd settled down he said, "I have asked Pastor Sullivan to say a prayer to start the contest." Pointing up to the balcony he said, "Pastor."

*"**Strong and faithful God, as we come together for this contest, we ask you to bless these athletes. Grant to these young men, strength to pursue excellence during this event. Keep them safe from serious injury and harm, instill in them respect for each other, and reward them for their perseverance. Today only one will receive the reward for victory. We beseech you Father, to lead us all to the rewards of Your kingdom where, You live and reign for ever and ever in victory.***

*****We pray this prayer in Your Son's name. Amen"*****

CHAPTER EIGHTEEN

A white chalk mark had been drawn on the ground in the center of the ring. The marshal said, "Gentlemen let me explain the Cornish rules one last time. Each round will start when both fighters toe the mark placed on the ground here." Pointing down at the ground. "A round will last until one fighter goes down, whether it is by knock down or if he slips and falls if one fighter goes to the ground that round is over. You are to go back to your neutral corner for one minute. Mr. Worthington," pointing to the banker sitting at a neutral corner of the ring, "will be the time keeper, when he says time each fighter will come back to the mark and when both fighters have toed the mark that round begins. I will allow no hitting below the belt, no biting, not gouging of the eyes no pulling of the hair. Do you understand the rules?"

Both fighters nodded yes.

The marshal stepped back and said, "Let the contest begin."

Colleen heard Marlene draw in her breath.

Jud had parked a wagon near the ring and had set up shop in the bed of the wagon. He was taking all bets. When the fight started he was still giving three to one odds on Grady. Sitting up in the wagon he could see over the crowd gathered near the ring. Jud had two heavily armed guards standing on either side of the window he had built at the back of the covered wagon, to use as a betting window.

⊨+ +⊨

As Grady's toe touched the mark Lonnie slugged him. The blow spun him around and he landed hard on his left side in the dirt.

"Round." The marshal said, "Back to your corners for one minute."

Grady's head rang like a church bell, he felt a flush creeping into his face when he heard several people in the crowd laughing.

"Grady this ain't no church picnic, it's a fight. You've got to be ready the minute you walk into the ring," Jacob said. "You're alright. You just got your bell rung a little bit that's all."

Mr. Worthington called, "Time."

This time Grady was ready. Lonnie tried the same thing again. Grady deflected his right with his left hand and sent his own right. It caught Lonnie on the jaw and spun him around, but he did not go down. He spun completely around and slammed his right fist into Grady's left side of his ribs so hard Grady was almost certain a rib had broken.

Grady backed off to catch his breath and Lonnie bore in. Swinging right hand over left as fast as he could. Grady managed to block most of the punches but a few got through.

Grady ducked under the barrage and whipped a right and left to Lonnie's bread basket as fast as he could.

This time Lonnie backed off. Grady thought *okay you don't like 'em down low.*

Lonnie faked a right and caught Grady with a wicked left that drew blood from a cut over Grady's right eye. Then he tried to follow up with a right that Grady slipped inside of the punch and snapped a right upper cut of his own that caught Lonnie on the chin and he stumbled back. Got his feet tangled up and fell on his backside.

"Round." the marshal said.

Jacob started working on the cut over his eye and said, "You did a lot better this round. Remember we've got---ten more rounds to go. Take your time, conserve your energy. He is real anxious so let him wear himself out."

"Jacob, that big dude can punch like a mule can kick."

"Don't stand toe to toe and trade punches with him. If you do you'll lose. Hit and weave, hit and dodge become a moving target. Tire him out. "

"Time."

Round three was brutal, both fighters giving everything they had to the battle. Each man absorbing punishing punches. Grady could feel his arms getting tired. Lonnie caught him with a left hook that shook him then followed up with a right cross and Grady's feet flew up. The next thing he knew he heard the referee say, five--- six. Oh no, he's counting. Grady rolled over and crawled over to his corner.

CHAPTER NINETEEN

The crowd was going wild, people were screaming, some for Grady some for Lonnie. People were showing up between each round wanting to bet some more money. The money on Grady was drying up so Jud raised the odds to four to one. Money started coming back in on Grady. Jud knew he could well afford to pay off the bets on Lonnie as long as he could get the suckers to bet on Grady.

There are two beautiful redheads sitting up there on the balcony that didn't know it but they are homeless, and broke. I'm going to win it all today.

"Time."

Grady spit out a mouth full of water and toed the mark. As soon as Lonnie's toe touched the mark Grady whipped a wicked right fist into his stomach. With an ooof, the crowd heard the air expelled from Lonnie's lungs. Lonnie stumbled back but he did not go down. Grady could hear the roar of the crowd. They were loving the action in the ring.

When Grady tried to move in Lonnie grabbed him and bear hugged him then head butted him smashing his nose. Blood exploded from Grady's face.

Marlene cover her eyes. "Oh I can't stand to see him get hurt."

Grady reached up and wiped the blood off his face with his left hand. When Lonnie came in with the intent to finish him off he threw all his might into a punch that caught Lonnie right over his heart. Dropped him flat in the dirt.

"Round."

When Grady got to his corner doctor Baker was there, "Let me look at you." He took two cotton balls out of his bag and stuffed one up each side of Grady's nose. You will have to breathe out of your mouth now. When this's over I'll set your nose, it's broken."

The next six rounds were brutal. Grady got knocked down five out of the next six rounds. Each time the referee asked him if he wanted to quit.

He said "NO. "

Now it was time for round eleven, Jacob said, "Grady, I think you should let me throw in the white towel, you're all used up, and you're out of fuel. There's no reason to go back out there and take any more beating. It needs to be over."

Grady's eyes were almost swollen shut, his lips were so cut and bruised he could barely speak but he said, "No. See those people out there that bet their money on me? I can't let them down."

"Grady you've been sick. You don't have your strength back. Today's not the day to be foolish. I'm going to throw the towel in."

Mr. Worthington called, "Time."

CHAPTER TWENTY

The crowd went wild when Grady grabbed the white towel out of Jacob's hand and threw it into the crowd.

Grady swayed a little as he walked back to the mark in the center of the ring. Lonnie sensing Grady was weak decided to go for the quick finish. He threw his Sunday punch and caught Grady coming in. Except Lonnie was getting so tired himself, to Grady it felt like a slap.

Grady grabbed Lonnie and clenched. Holding on just to gain a few seconds reprieve. The referee stepped in and pushed them apart. Both fighters looked punch drunk. Grady faked a right cross to Lonnie's chin then dropped his fist down and slammed it into his stomach. Lonnie staggered back a few steps. Grady started after him to finish him off, both fighters looked like they had been run through a meat grinder, both were covered in blood and bruises.

Grady swung with all he could put behind the punch, this one should end it right here. Lonnie jumped back and Grady missed. In so doing Grady lost his balance and fell into the ropes. He hung on to the ropes and did not hit the ground stopping the round.

Lonnie saw Grady holding onto the rope and moved in for the knock out. Grady saw him coming and kicked out with his left foot tripping Lonnie who landed face down in the dirt.

"Round," the marshal called.

When Grady staggered back to his corner Doctor Baker said, "I don't care what you say I'm stopping this right now and stepped over the ropes and said, "Folks you have seen one heck of a fight. You sure got you dollars' worth today but it's over. I'm stopping the fight, both fighters are willing to go on but it makes no sense, it's over. Some of the crowd were cheering some were booing.

Lonnie had made it back to the mark. The marshal lifted his hand in the air and said, "Lonnie I think you'll agree Grady fought one heck of a fight. Congratulations you are the winner." They looked around and Grady was slumped to the ground in his corner.

Doctor Baker said, "Get him over to my house."

⟞⟝

Jud strutted into the saloon and said, "Drinks are on me boys. Set'em up bar keep."

"That's why it's called gamblin' boys. I didn't have any way of knowing who was gonna win any more than you did. You'll have to admit they did a lot of fightin'."

Someone yelled, "Hell you orta buy, you got all our money."

"Barkeep just keep setting'em up. The whole party's on me tonight. We had ourselves a hell-of-a fight."

A chorus of raucous yells sounded around the room.

When the entire crowd was getting drunk, Jud pulled his number one man to one side. "Go easy on the liquor, I want you in the saddle at first light. I want you to go to El Paso and bring back as many fightin' men as you can find, who know how to use a gun. Tell'em I'm paying fightin' wages."

CHAPTER TWENTY-ONE

Grady woke up and looked around. Where am I? How did I get here? He looked down and his hands were bandaged up. When he touched his face it was bandaged too. Then it came to him, the fight, what happened, who won?

Someone moved beside the bed. He looked and Marlene was standing there. He blinked. She said, "Well at least you are still alive."

He tried to sit up and groaned, he hurt everywhere. He said, "Are you sure?"

"Sure of what?"

"That I'm still alive. "

"I wasn't sure when they brought you in here. If you're hurting you're still alive."

"Then I must be plenty alive." Then he gasped.

"What's the matter do you want me to run get the doctor?"

"No, I feel so bad. A lot of people lost a lot of money betting on me and I let'em down."

The next thing he knew, Dr. Baker, Pastor and Mrs. Sullivan, Colleen and Marlene were all there.

"Doctor Baker said if you hadn't been sick all week you would've won. "

Pastor Sullivan and Mrs. Sullivan insisted Colleen and Marlene come to their house after the fight.

Mrs. Sullivan said, "Come on in ladies. I have some sun tea already brewed and it has been sitting in the cold spring water all the time we were watching the fight. Everybody sit down at the table while I get it."

Pastor Sullivan said, "Well girls what did you think of the fight?"

"It was awful." Marlene said, "I didn't know they would actually get hurt." Tears started to well up in the corners of her eyes.

"It was a lot more brutal than I thought." Colleen said, "It was my first prize fight and I think my last."

Mrs. Sullivan came back in carrying a large pickle jar. She sat four glasses on the table and poured each full of cool tea.

The pastor sipped and said, "I declare Mrs. Sullivan you do make the best sun tea."

"Girls I have some bad news, to share with you."

"What could be worse than somebody murdering our father?" Colleen said.

"Nothing could be worse than that dear, but this is almost as bad."

"What?"

"The telegraph operator has informed me that Jud wired a lawyer in Austin and had him file the papers to take possession of Hill Valley Ranch. He received a wire just before the fight giving him title to the ranch. He now owns the ranch."

The two sisters looked at each other. Marlene said, "What are we gonna do? We don't have a home to go back to?"

Mrs. Sullivan said, "We want you two to stay with us until this can get sorted out. God will provide."

Pastor Sullivan said, "**1 Corinthians 10:13 - God keeps his promise, and he will not allow you to be tested beyond your power to** remain firm; at this time you are put to the test, he will give you the strength to endure it."

"First let's pray and then we plan. Too many times we plan first and when the plans don't work out we start to pray."

"Holy God, you have called us on this journey to be faithful and to follow obediently

We know You have ways in making everything well according to Your timing and plan. Lord there are many things in this world that we do not understand.

There are too many uncertainties and uncontrolled elements. Lord we are asking for contentment in You for full submission to Your will. Give us the strength to trust in Your plans for our lives. Today Lord we place our two young friends wholly in Your care. May their hearts and minds ever rest secure in You.

Lord the future right now looks long and dark for Colleen and Marlene, but we know that you love them and you will send an angel to watch over each of our young friends. We ask for your hand to be involved and see them through.

In Your son's name we pray,
Amen."

"Now here is what I think we can do immediately."

CHAPTER TWENTY-TWO

G rady had difficulty climbing up to the hay loft when he got back to the livery stable. He was sore all over especially his hands, arms, shoulders and rib cage. All of which was needed to climb a ladder up to the hay loft.

Knot dutifully took a position as sentry at the bottom of the ladder leading to the loft. Knot was going to make sure that nobody disturbed Grady while he slept.

Grady lay there in the hay staring at the rafters in the barn. He had lost everything. Going back to work tomorrow was going to be brutal with all these aches and pains. Then he grinned and his mouth hurt. "At least ole Lonnie will be hurting almost as much as me. I did wallop him a little."

Then another thought came to him. *I did bet $25.00 on Lonnie so I'll at least have eat 'en money. Darn I lost the money I put down on the wagon. That was a good one too.*

Then he said out loud, "Grady your first venture into the business world sure was a flop." He tried to turn over and pain racked through him, "a painful flop'." Grady was feeling a lot of pain in his body, but the deepest hurt was inside. He was sick and injured and totally alone in the whole world he didn't have one person but himself. Tears trickled down his cheek as he lay his head in the hay.

⇥⊹ ⊹⇤

Jud came to Pastor Sullivan's home Monday morning. When Mrs. Sullivan came to the door he politely held his hat in his hands and said, "Good morning Mrs. Sullivan. I would like to speak with Colleen and Marlene. I have business to discuss with them."

"Please wait right here. I will inquire if they are up to seeing anyone yet."

Mrs. Sullivan walked back into the kitchen and said, "Jud is at the door asking to talk to you. Shall I send him away?"

Colleen said, "No we may as well find out what he has to say. We'll meet him in the parlor."

Mrs. Sullivan opened the door and said, "Mr. Rawlins come into the parlor. The ladies will talk with you there."

Mrs. Sullivan showed Jud into the parlor and politely left the room, giving the girls some privacy.

Jud said, "I guess you heard I have taken possession of the Hill Valley Ranch."

"No, you stole the ranch from Marlene and me."

"Well we don't have to be adversaries. Here is my offer. Colleen, I'll marry you and then we'll share the ranch together. We'll pay for Marlene to return to finishing school. Or if that is not acceptable I will marry Marlene and then, she and I'll share the ranch and we'll provide a home for her spinster sister."

Colleen said, "Let me tell you something Jud and you listen well. We know you are probably the murdering skunk that slipped into a paralyzed man's room and murdered him. From this day on I will personally be carrying a gun and if you ever come close to Marlene again. I will kill you. Do you understand me?"

"Are you threatening me, you little hell-cat?"

"No sir, I am not. I am making you a solemn promise. So I suggest you get up and get out of this house immediately."

"Well just so you know I own Hill Valley Ranch and everything on it. You've got nothing. You need me. You'll come to your senses as soon as you realize that." He jammed his hat back on his head and marched out the door.

⇥ ⇤

Grady ate breakfast slowly because his jaw was too sore to eat fast. When May came to refill his coffee, He said, "May I'm sorry you bet on me and I let you down."

"Honey, you didn't let me down. You put up a heck-of-a fight. He was getting tired. I still think you might have knocked him out if the doc hadn't stopped the fight. Besides I didn't bet but $50.00 on you and I did more business Saturday, with that crowd in town, than I normally do in a month. No need to apologize to me. Just let me know when you get ready to do another one."

"May, that ain't gonna happen. I'm gonna find a safer way to make money."

"How many tickets did y'all sell?"

"I don't even know. The last I heard was that crazy Ronnie bet all the ticket money on me because the odds were so good."

"Do you mean you two beat the devil out of each other for nothing?"

"Sounds that way."

"Maybe you two should whoop ole Ronnie, so he can get something out of it too."

"If it's all the same to you I ain't whooping nothing but these eggs."

She smiled and patted him on the shoulder, he winced.

Grady sat staring into the coffee cup, *I wonder if I'm going to have-ta sleep in a barn for the rest of my life?*

⊨+ +⊫

Ronnie and Lonnie walked into the feed mill. Mr. Johnson said, "Lonnie, am I gonna get any work out of you today?"

"Probably not as much as usual. They say I won, but I sure don't feel like it. That dang Grady can hit like a thunder bolt. I hurt all over. The bad part is we bet all our money on Grady because they was giving three to one odds. So we figured if he won we'd get a lot of money."

"Guys, that's a sucker play. You knew he'd been sick all week. That's why they were giving the odds. They knew he'd been sick so they figured there was no way he could win."

"They may have knowed it but they shore didn't tell him."

"Have y'all seen him this morning?"

"Only from a distance. He was going into May's when I was coming across the street."

"Well come and find me when he gets here I've got something to tell you boys."

CHAPTER TWENTY-THREE

The sheriff walked into the marshal's office. "You got anything on the killin' yet."

"No I haven't, my deputies and I have talked to everybody in town and nobody saw anybody climb in or out of that window. Nobody saw anybody even walk down that side of the house."

"You got a pretty good hunch that Jud did it though, don't cha."

"Yeah I do but I can't come up with a motive. He had the note already and the old man couldn't pay it. All he had to do was file it and claim the ranch. There is no reason why he would need to kill the old man. He has been trying to pressure the oldest daughter into marrying him. How would killing her father help him get her to marry him?" The marshal said.

"Hum, maybe he thought if she was homeless and fatherless she would feel she had no choice except to marry him."

"Sheriff, it just don't add up. I need a motive. He already had that play going. There has to be something new that we don't know about."

"What is his alibi? Where was he that night?"

"He was in the saloon all evening," the marshal said.

"Have you interviewed the people who work in the saloon?"

The marshal thought for a moment then said, "No I haven't, I've been concentrating on trying to find someone who saw something in or around that house."

"You know marshal, people who commit murder are the lowest lowlife on earth."

"Yeah, and especially this murder. The old man was paralyzed on one side and he still managed to put up a fight. That is a coward in the first degree who will sneak into a cripple man's room and suffocate him with a pillow. I would feel better if the low life had stuck a gun in the window and blew his brains out."

"Well me too. That way the old man wouldn't have had to suffer. You know struggling to get some air in your lungs has got to be a horrible way to die. You are lying there knowing full well somebody is doing it to you on purpose. Sad."

"It has been keeping me awake at night thinking about it. We know how he did it. We know when he did it. As weak as the old man was anyone could have done it. So it gets down to who had a motive." The marshal said.

"You know what they say, murder is done for one of two things, sex or money."

"Or power. In this case he has plenty of money or at least he appears too. As much time as he spends with the gals in the saloon he's getting plenty of sex. What am I missing?"

"Well keep digging. Somebody saw something or heard something that they don't even know is significant but it's the key. You keep digging and somebody's neck is gonna get stretched. If me or any of my deputies can help just holler."

"Thanks, I hope I find it before it drives me crazy. We ain't never had an out-n-out murder before. People get shot or stabbed all the time but murdered. Naw."

Jacob walked into May's and saw Grady eating breakfast. Pulling up a chair across from him, Jacob said, "Grady do you have a gun?"

"No."

"After work today come out to my place. I've got an extra six-shooter. I'll give ya, and I'll teach ya how to shoot it."

"Father O'Malley wouldn't let us boys have guns out at the ranch."

"Well you ain't living on the ranch any more so you are gonna need one. Especially if you get that freight wagon you've been talking about. There's still plenty of Indians from down south of the border doing raids up here in this part of Texas. We lawmen ain't caught all the owl hoots yet."

Later that day Grady showed up at Jacob's home. Jacob was sharpening an axe on a grinding wheel. "Grady you are just in time. Get down off that horse and come turn this wheel while I hold the axe to it. It's hard to get a keen edge with one hand and turn the wheel with the other."

Grady tied the horse Bledsoe had loaned him to the top rail on the corral. "Jacob you got a nice place here."

"Takes a lot of work to keep it up. I appreciate the marshal giving me a job, 'cause this place don't make enough money to keep a jaybird alive yet. But I love it. When I get home I love the peace and quiet out here."

The ringing sound of steel on grind stone could be heard all around. Jacob touched the edge of the axe and said, "That'll chop some wood." Turned and buried the head of the axe into a log laying nearby. "Grady always leave your axe buried in a piece of wood it'll keep the blade from getting rusty.

"Come on up to the house, let me introduce you to the missus. We'll get a drink of water and I'll get that six-shooter for ya."

When they reached the back door of the house, Jacob stepped in and said, "Come on in."

When Grady stepped through the door he saw an attractive young woman in a flower sack apron working at the stove.

Jacob said, "Molly this here is Grady. You remember the fellow that was in that prize fight the other day."

Molly smiled and wiped her hands on the apron, then extended her right hand, "Hello Grady, I see most of your bruises are clearing up. Are you okay now?"

Grady was holding his hat in his right hand and when he went to shift it to his left hand it slipped out of his fingers and rolled across the kitchen floor. He stumbled to catch the fleeing hat and ignored the right hand extended in greeting. Just as he caught up with the hat he realized how rude he had been, turning red in the face he blurted out, "Sorry ma'am."

Molly was smiling, Jacob was laughing. Grady stood there gripping the wily hat in both hands to make sure it didn't escape again.

Jacob reached over on the cupboard and picked up a six-shooter and holster belt, "Come on Grady before you and that hat wreck the kitchen."

Molly still smiling said, "Nice to meet you Grady."

Grady jammed the hat down on his head and said, "Yes ma'am," then escaped out the back door.

They walked down past the barn. Jacob stopped and opened the cylinder on the gun and shook six bullets out. He shoved the now empty gun back in the leather holster and handed it to Grady. "Buckle the belt around your middle with the pistol hanging on your right side."

Now see that tall straight pine tree? I want you to practice pulling that gun out and keeping the end of the barrel lined up on that tree all the way up to eye level. Like this." He took out his own gun and smoothly kept the end of the barrel pointed at the tree all the way to eye level.

Grady pulled the pistol out of the holster and aimed it at the tree. It felt awkward the first time he tried it.

"That was good Grady. Now I want you to do it ten times's in a row and try to do it faster each time."

Jacob watched, "You're getting more comfortable. Now I want you to click the trigger as soon as the gun gets eye level."

"I don't have any bullets in it."

"I know we're going to get used to the motion and feel of the trigger pull before we go to wasting any ammunition. Now do that ten times and try to do it faster each time."

"Grady you have the best hand and eye coordination, I've ever seen. You have a natural dexterity that is amazing to watch. Hand me the gun."

Jacob took the gun and inserted the bullets into the cylinder. Handing it back he said, "Do it exactly the same way. Now let's see if you hit the pine tree when you pull the trigger."

Grady's first shot missed. "Do you know why you missed?"

"Yaeh, when I pulled the trigger I pulled the end of the barrel, off the tree."

"That's right. So this time don't pull the trigger squeeze the trigger."

CHAPTER TWENTY-FOUR

Colleen stepped out of the mercantile and met two men dressed in business suits, "One of the men took off his hat and said, "Pardon me miss are you Colleen O'Shanity?"

"Yes, and whom shall I presume you to be?"

Both men had removed their hats, "My name is Miliband and this is Mr. Dunston. We have some business to discuss with you." Pointing to a door that said Joseph (Joe) Thacker, Attorney at Law on it, he said, "We just came from the attorney's office. It is a co-incidence that we met you here, because we were coming to find you. Will you please step into the attorney's office so we can discuss some business with you?"

"Gentlemen this is highly irregular. To accost a lady on the street and ask her to stop and talk business with, especially as I have no business. We just lost our father and he left us nothing."

"I understand, I think you will find Mr. Thacker the attorney is quite reputable and capable of representing your best interest, even if he is just out of law school. Please step in and hear what we have to say."

⚊⊹ ⊹⚊

Marlene looked up and saw Jud getting off a horse and going into the café. She thought I am pretty brazen to walk into a café alone but here goes. Let's go see what Jud has to say today.

When she walked into May's, Jud stood up and said, "Hello Princess. I was certain that this morning's sunrise was the most beautiful thing I would see all day, and then you walked in. Please have breakfast with me."

"Jud you are a fraud."

"No my dear I am a lover of beauty, the beauty of nature, beautiful horseflesh, a beautiful bird, and of course beautiful women."

"I seriously doubt there is any truth in any of those words."

"You my dear should be a little more courteous and considerate, I have not finished what I intended to say."

"Well in that case excuse me, please go on Mr. Rawlins."

"Very well I accept your apology. Now Marlene, my dear, we'll get back to what I was about to say about beauty. We can pass over the beauty of nature because we are both aware of it. We don't need to invest time in talking about the beauty of birds as they are all around us. As to the beauty of horseflesh that is in the eye of the beholder. Any horse lucky enough to have you riding upon its back would be instantly beautiful."

"Jud that is amazing. Just for an instant there I thought you were sincere."

"Oh Marlene dear, when I speak of your radiant beauty, I'm very sincere. Look around this room, every man in this place is having difficulty concentrating on his food. In fact that cowhand over there has missed his mouth twice trying to shovel food in and stare at you at the same time."

"Let's get serious for a few minutes. I want to marry you and make you the queen of the most famous home in Texas. I will soon own not one but several ranches. We'll build an empire out of these plains. Then I'll become governor of the state of Texas and you my dear will make a beautiful first lady. I can see you now radiant in splendid gowns with your flaming red hair and beautiful green eyes. You will make the most breath taking first lady this state has ever known."

"Jud you make it all sound so grand. How do you plan to accomplish all of these things?"

"That is business and a beautiful head like yours need not be filled with trivial things like business."

"You make this sound like a business transaction. In all this you haven't mentioned love even once."

"Oh no my dear. I was smitten the minute I saw you step off that stage.

"Why do you think I raced over to carry your bags that first evening you came into town? Haven't you ever heard of love at first sight? Marlene the feeling was so good it was almost painful. Just walking beside you and breathing in the air you exhaled, then to listen to the melody of your sweet voice. You are a dream in motion every time I see you."

"What about Colleen?"

"I thought Colleen was the most gorgeous woman in the world until you stepped off that stage. She is your sister and we will see that she is well taken care of until she marries."

"Mr. Rawlins, you do give a girl some things to think about."

"There's nothing to think about, let's go see that preacher man and get married right away."

"Let me think about it Jud. It's a big decision on my part. You have had time to think and plan. I need a little time. If I get married I want a real wedding with flowers and candles and bunting."

"Very well my dear, you shall have the grandest wedding this area has ever seen, if you want them I'll ship in a mariachi band from El Paso."

Marlene laughed and said, "I definitely would not want a mariachi band from El Paso."

"Then you just say what you do want and I'll make it happen. I'll get you a blues band from New Orleans, if that will make you happy. You marry me and I'll spoil you."

The next morning, Marlene sat staring out the window. She had never felt so alone and confused in all her life. The pastor and Mrs. Sullivan were wonderful people and made them feel welcome in their home. She thought we can't live here forever. I love my sister. Maybe I should marry Jud. He is rather handsome. He now has daddy's ranch so I would have a home and we could see that Colleen had a home.

She bowed her head and said, *"Lord what should I do? You said we should lay down our life for others like you gave up your life for us. Does that mean I should lay down my life for my sister? Oh Lord, I am so confused. Please show me something to point me in the direction you want me to go. I don't want to marry the man who may have killed our daddy. Then again I don't want to see my sister destitute and homeless. What should I do Lord?*

Amen

CHAPTER TWENTY-FIVE

The marshal took one more opportunity to examine the area outside the window that the killer would have climbed through to murder Mr. O'Shanity.

As he was standing there the sun rays reflected off something shiny in the dust below the window. Stooping down to look closer he saw a tiny gold link off a chain lying in the dust. Picking it up and balancing it on the tip of his index finger he thought, *this is a link out of a necklace. Why would a link out of a woman's necklace be out here in the dust?* He took a cigarette paper out of his pocket and wrapped the tiny gold link in it.

"I don't know what that link is from, but I have suspicion it's an important find."

The marshal walked over to the jeweler and said, "Mr. Moskowitz do you recognize what kind if neckless this came from?"

"It's a common design. A little larger than most though."

"Do you remember making one for some lady that this could have come from?"

"Marshal why all the questions about one little scrap of chain?"

"Oh I found it lying in the sand and thought some lady would like to get it back so her locket chain could be fixed."

The Whitley's ran a small dry land farm along the east side of Turkey creek. Mr. Whitley was forking hay to his horses late in the evening when Jud rode into his yard.

Jud said, "Whitley, the Hill-Valley Ranch has been missing cattle. I think you have been feeding your family off my cattle. Furthermore you have been digging irrigation ditches into Turkey creek and siphoning off water that my cows need, to irrigate those miserable crops of yours. I'm here to buy you out. I'll give you $100.00 cash for this place lock stock and barrel. Then you can gather up your personal goods and that bunch of brats of yours, get in a wagon and go find a place somewhere else."

"You're a crazy man to ride in here and talk like that. I have never stolen anything from any man ever. My place is not for sale."

Jud whipped out a six-shooter and shot him down in front of his wife and children. Then threw $100.00 down on the ground and said, "I want you all off here before tomorrow night."

Two nights later the Nicholson's barn caught fire and burned up all of the hay they had stored up for winter. The next day Jud rode into their yard and told them they had two days to get off his range.

The next night someone shot and killed their milk cow.

When Jud showed up the next day and offered them $100.00 to vacate, they took it.

The attorney said, "Gentlemen step out in the waiting area and let me talk to my client for a minute."

"No problem, we'll wait right out here."

When the door closed the lawyer said, "Colleen, here's the deal. The railroad wants to lay tracks across the Hill-Valley Ranch and they offered to pay your father $1,000.00 for the right-of-way lease. He accepted their offer, they shook hands on the deal. They were supposed to come back the next morning and bring him a draft for $1,000.00. He agreed to sign the lease."

"Then someone killed him before he could sign it." Colleen said,

"Right, but the hand shake deal was witnessed by the doctor. Even though Jud now has possession of the ranch, which in its self is suspicious, the rail road is willing to pay you the $1,000.00. As the executor of his estate, you can sign the lease and Jud has no choice except to honor it. I'll charge $100.00 for my services which I'm sure the railroad will agree to pay for you."

"Does Jud know about this?"

"Yes, we informed him last night."

"That is wonderful. When would I get the money?"

"I'll draw up the lease today and y'all can come back Monday. They will give you a bank draft as soon as you sign the papers.

Mr. Thacker that is wonderful, now I can pay for Marlene's next year at school."

CHAPTER TWENTY-SIX

J acob walked into the marshal's office Monday morning. "I understand you've been teaching Grady how to shoot."

"Yes I have and I'll tell you something else. That boy has the best dexterity I have ever seen. His hand and eye coordination is amazing. He hit the target four out of six shots the first time he fired a gun. He is fast too, if he practices a little more he is going to be scary fast."

"Maybe we better hire him. We'll make him a lawman so we don't have to face him as an outlaw," The marshal said.

"Told him to go out of town and practice drawing and firing his gun without any bullets in it every evening this week. Saturday I'll have him come back out to my place and see how he is doing."

"Well that's good because he needs to know how to handle a gun right. In these times. I wouldn't want to ride outside of town without a gun. Too many road agents and Indians still around. I got a wire yesterday where somebody held up a stage over at Sweetwater Falls and killed the guard."

"I'll let you know how Grady's doing. Has the sheriff said anything to you about some strange things going on out in the county?"

"All we talked about was a suspicious killing Jud got involved in. Apparently Jud went over to try and buy out a sod farmer and got into an argument and the farmer tried to stick him with a pitch fork and Jud shot him. At least that's Jud's story. Anyway they couldn't arrest him or charge him with anything."

"Well as long as he keeps it out in the county it's not our problem. Have you got any leads on who killed Mr. O'Shanity?"

The marshal pulled the cigarette paper out of his desk drawer, "I found this link off a gold necklace chain in the sand outside of the window that the murderer climbed in to kill Mr. O'Shanity. I took it over to the jeweler and he said it is a common type chain link but he also said it appears to be larger than the size most women like to wear."

Jud called his men together, "Boys I want you to round up a thousand head of beef and drive them to the stockyards in Fort Worth. Start with those closest but if you get some with other brands on'em I don't care because they are all gonna be mine pretty soon."

"Wait a minute Jud I thought we was getting hired on as gun slingers not cow maids."

"You are getting paid $100.00 a month. You'll do whatever I tell you. You were all hired because you are fighting men. This drive won't take but about ten or twelve days to get to Fort Worth. You can layover and brace the tiger if you want but get right back. As soon as I get some more operating capital out of the sale of these beefs you'll see what you have been hired for. We won't have to drive to Fort Worth anymore because the railroad will be here in a few more weeks. Next time I want to ship some we can do it from here."

Sunday morning Grady got up, whetted up his razor and shaved by looking at his reflection in the watering tank. He put on his clean shirt and went to church. As he stepped in he saw Colleen and Marlene sitting on the third bench, "Do you mind if I sit here?"

Marlene smiled and said, "No, please sit."

All during church Grady looked straight ahead but the only thing he saw, out of the corner of his eye, was the prettiest girl he had ever seen.

The pastor's sermon was taken from Psalm 72:12 "For he will deliver the needy who cry out, the afflicted who have no one to help."

Then he recited: Psalm 34:6

"This poor man called, and the LORD heard him; He saved him out of all his troubles."

Colleen thought, *yes Lord. I trust in you. I thank you for the $1,000.00 I am to receive tomorrow. Help me to use it wisely. So I can support my sister and myself until we can marry the men you chose for us rather than one for convenience and safety sake.*

As soon as church was over the pastor's wife came to Grady and said, "Grady, I have cooked a large roast. Would you come and have lunch with us? I am sure Colleen and Marlene would not mind having a handsome young man join us for lunch."

Grady felt his ears start to feel flush.

Colleen said, "Grady you would be a fool to say no to Mrs. Sullivan's invitation. She is without a doubt the best cook in the territory."

Grady twisted is hat in his hands said, "Thank you ma'am. I don't want Colleen and Marlene to think of me as a fool. So I would love to try some of that roast."

The pastor walked up and said, "Are we going to have another guest?"

Lunch was delicious. Marlene asked, "Pastor, do you really believe that stuff that says God will hear the needy and do something to help them if they ask him to?"

"Yes, Marlene I do. Sometimes we ask for one thing and he gives us something different, that is actually better. God allows evil to exist in this world and we have to overcome it. Like Job did, but if you remember the story, in the end Job was better off than at the beginning. God didn't cause someone to kill your father and Jud to take your home. But if you keep your trust in him I promise you he will see you through these times and you will be fine in the end."

After a little while the conversation turned to Grady. Mrs. Sullivan asked, "Grady why did you agree to that awful fight with Lonnie Higgins?"

"Well it was my idea. You see, Mr. Johnson told me there was a need for another freight company in the territory that was reliable. It seems that the one we have likes to drink a lot and gets drunk. Then doesn't show up when he is supposed to pick up a load. I asked Mr. Bledsoe how much money it would cost to buy a freight wagon and a team of mules. He said $500.00. So I thought up the idea of a prize fight to make enough money to buy a team and wagon."

The pastor said, "That was a pretty good business strategy Grady. How much of the purse were you supposed to get and how much was Lonnie supposed to get?"

"I offered to give Lonnie and Ronnie one half and I would keep one half since it was my idea and I did all the promoting. I never thought about getting sick just six days before the event."

"Did you get enough to buy your wagon?"

"No sir, Ronnie was supposed to collect the money from selling tickets. Then Jud started offering three to one odds on me so Ronnie bet all of the money he had collected on me. And as you know I lost."

"Did Jud know you were sick," Colleen asked?

"Yes, I guess he saw me when I left the doctor's house and I was running a high fever."

"What day was that?"

"Monday."

"That was the same day he started giving three to one odds." The reverend said. "He knew you would not be well enough to fight twelve rounds by Saturday. You have to give him credit that was shrewd on his part."

Mrs. Sullivan asked, "What are your plans now Grady?"

"Ma'am, I don't know. A man could become wealthy right now if he had a good team and wagon. It will take me a year to save up enough money to buy a wagon. Before then someone else will probably step in and do it. It's just an opportunity lost."

Colleen asked, "How much could you make with one wagon if you had it?"

"Mr. Bledsoe said, I could make about $60.00 a load so if I did one load a day I would earn about $300.00 a week. Of course I'd have to buy feed for the mules and keep the wagon repaired but I would still make a lot of money."

"Do you think you can get a load every day?"

"I could get a load a day from Mr. Johnson. There are other loads that can be had too. In fact I've got an idea. I would get two teams of mules and tie one behind the wagon. They wouldn't be puling any load so when the first team got tired, I'd switch and that way I might be able to do two loads in a day some days."

The pastor spoke up and said, "Grady that sounds pretty smart because if you got in mud or deep sand you could move the back two up front and have all four pulling."

"Yes sir, but it doesn't matter. Long before I can save up $500.00 that opportunity will be gone. I'll just have to save my money and keep my eyes open for another opportunity to go into business."

Grady looked at Colleen and Marlene and said, "I am sorry ladies, I didn't mean to bore you with all this business talk."

CHAPTER TWENTY-SEVEN

Colleen arrived at the lawyer's office Monday morning sharply at 10:00 o'clock, the time of her appointment to meet with the railroad men. They were already there waiting for her.

"Good morning Miss O'Shanity, nice to see you again." The railroad men said in unison.

She smiled and stuck out her hand in greeting, "Nice to see you as well, and you Mr. Thacker."

Mr. Thacker said, "Good morning Miss O'Shanity. I have drawn up the lease papers we discussed in our last meeting. If you would like to read them you may. I think you will find they are straight forward and in order. You in effect are leasing the right of way for the railroad to run its track across the Hill-Valley ranch for a distance of five miles starting at the point of the east property line and continuing approximately west for five miles to the west property line. You shall be paid a onetime sum of $1,000.00 today and the gentlemen from the railroad have agreed to pay the modest attorney's fee for you," Offering the papers to her he said, "Would you like to read them yourself before signing them?"

"No since you are my attorney I trust you. I do have a question?"

"Okay what is your question?"

"My question is for these gentlemen." indicating the railroad men.

"Yes ma'am."

"You are aware that Jud Rawlins now has ownership of the Hill-Valley ranch, is that correct?"

"Yes our attorneys are aware of that fact. However we have acquired a sworn statement from the doctor stating that he did in fact witness us making a deal and shaking hands to seal the deal with your father before his untimely death. We are deeply sorry for your loss. Now, since you are the guardian of his estate, our attorney's will accept your signature in lieu of your fathers. This deal was made prior to Mr. Rawlins filing a quick claim deed at the state capital. The lease stands and we are prepared to place in your hands a bank draft for $1,000.00 at this time."

Colleen turned to her attorney and said, "Mr. Thacker, do you have ink and a writing instrument?"

He dipped an ink pen in the ink well and handed it to her. "Miss O'Shanity, there are two copies please sign both. One for these gentlemen and one I will keep on file for you."

Both railroad agents stepped forward and signed each copy of the lease. One of them reached into his jacket pocket and produced a long white envelope and handed it to Colleen. "Miss O'Shanity you will find a bank draft inside for $1,000.00 payable to you. It is a pleasure to do business with a lady as beautiful as you. Have a good day."

She took the envelope, peeked inside and said, "Gentlemen it is a pleasure to do business with you. Good day."

As soon as they left the office Colleen said, "Can I hire you to do something else for me?"

The lawyer laid down his pencil and said, "Sure. What do you need?"

Sheriff Adams sat looking out the window and said, "I don't like the feeling I'm getting. Something bad is brewing and I don't like the way it feels."

"What are you thinking about Sheriff?"

"First there was that Whitley killin', the widow was so distraught she wasn't making any sense, but she kept saying Jud just rode up and shot her husband without warning. Then threw some money on the ground and rode off. She says Jud never said anything."

"You think she might be telling the truth?"

"I'm sure that's the way she remembers it, but when I got there I could see where Jud's horse had stood in one place and moved around a bit before he turned and rode away. So I know Jud didn't just ride up there and shoot the man and ride away without stopping to talk."

"Then there is the incident over at the Olsen's where somebody set fire to their barn and burned up all their hay. Then somebody came back the next night and killed their milk cow."

"I believe if I was Olsen I'd be sitting up nights guarding my hen house before they come back and killed my chickens."

"In each case they are forced to sell and Jud is the one who buys them out. Something just smells fishy."

"Don't forget Sheriff, we have been hearing rumors that he is hiring gunfighters and paying $100.00 a month per gun. Hey, that's a lot more than a deputy makes, maybe I could go over there and get a job."

The sheriff grinned and said, "Your problem is you can't hit a barn in broad daylight. You were hired for your brains and not your gun skills so I need you to start earning your pay and help me figure all this out."

"Didn't the marshal say that Jud was his number one suspect in the murder of Mr. O'Shanity?"

"Yes he did. I think I'll ride over there and see how he's coming with his investigation. See what he's learned."

An hour later sheriff Adams walked into the marshal's office.

"Well howdy sheriff, what brings you over here today. I hope you're not bringing me anymore crimes to solve. This murder of Mr. O 'Shanity is driving me crazy. I know there is something right under my nose that I'm missing but I don't know what it is."

Dragging up a chair the sheriff said, "Tell me what you've got so far."

The marshal told him about interviewing everybody on the street and nobody saw anything. Then he told him about the little gold chain link off a ladies neckless. Nothing fits.

"What about this Jud dude, is he still your number one suspect?"

"Well he would be except I can find no motive for him to kill the old man. He already had the mortgage on the old man's ranch. In fact he had an attorney in Austin file it the morning we found the old man dead."

"Don't you find that timing a little strange?"

"It is, but there again why kill the old man. He could've filed them papers even if the old man had been standing right beside him."

"I've got something strange going on, at least it feels strange. You know that same Jud gunned down a sod farmer the other day. It happened when Jud went over there and tried to buy him out. Then a few days later he tried to buy out another farmer and was turned down. That night the man's barn burned down, burning up all of his winter hay. Then the next night somebody sneaked back over there and killed his milk cow. Jud bought him out the next day."

"Sheriff you and I have been in the lawin' business too long to believe in coincidences. There's a skunk in the wood pile somewhere."

CHAPTER TWENTY-EIGHT

Colleen sent word to Grady that she wanted to see him.
After Grady got off work early today because they had all the
freight loaded by noon. He walked over to the pastor's house and
knocked on the door. Mrs. Sullivan opened the door, "Good afternoon Grady. Please come in. Colleen's in the parlor, she's waiting
to talk to you. Can I get you a glass of cold tea?"

"Yes ma'am that would be great."

Grady stepped into the parlor, Colleen rose as he entered, she
said, "Grady thank you for coming. Please sit down."

"You wanted to see me?"

"Grady, I was intrigued by your story about the freight business.
Can you tell me more?"

"What do you want to know?" Grady asked confused.

"How much money do you realistically think you could earn in
a month, or a year? What would you do with the money?"

Grady thought, that is a weird question. What would I do with
my money?

Grady relaxed and thought, *this is just a conversation with a beautiful young woman.* "Well, you have actually asked two questions. Let

me address the first one first. I realistically believe I can haul one load of freight every day except Sunday, of course. That would earn $250.00 to $300.00 a week, or between $1,000.00 and $1,200.00 in a month. Of course I'd have to pay for feed for the mules and make repairs to the wagons out of the money I collect. As to how I would spend the money. I would continue to sleep in the hay loft at the livery stable until I collected enough to purchase two more wagons. When I had three wagons and teams I would recruit three honest, sober, dependable drivers. Then I would purchase a piece of ground near town and build a wagon yard. On the grounds I would build a large building to use as a warehouse for freight coming in and going out."

"Surely by then you would no longer be sleeping in the hay loft?"

"No I would build an apartment in a corner of the warehouse for me to live. Of course these are only dreams. It would take me a year to save enough money to purchase a wagon and team. By then the opportunity will be gone. Someone else will have the contracts. It is fun to plan and dream."

"What if you had a partner who could give you the money right now?"

"Wow. That would be wonderful."

"How would you divide the money earned with your partner?"

"Colleen, before I answer that let me ask you a question."

"Alright."

"Do you know such a person? Who might be willing to partner in an adventure like this?"

"I do."

"Well in that case. I would be happy to enter into an agreement with such a partner. How the profits would be divided would depend on how much he would be willing to contribute to the building of the business. If he paid the money for the first team and wagon then he would be entitled to one half of the profits earned by that wagon for his investment and I would be entitled to one half because I would be doing all the driving of the wagon. "

"What about the other wagons you mentioned?"

Grady thought about that question for a minute then said, "If he took his share of the profits from the first wagon and kept it and I took my share and invested it in the new wagons. He would not have a share in my wagons. However, if he was willing to help build the business, if we each only took out an agreed amount to live on and allowed the rest of the profits to stay in the business and used them to purchase all new equipment, then he would be an equal partner in everything the business owned."

"What if it wasn't a man?"

"What?"

"I said what if your partner wasn't a man?"

"Colleen, I don't understand. What are you talking about?"

"What if your partners were Marlene and me?"

Grady's eyes widened, "How could that be? I thought Jud took your ranch."

"My daddy made a deal with the railroad before," her voice broke.

"Colleen, I'm so sorry."

She dried her eyes in a handkerchief and cleared her throat, "He made a deal with the railroad to lease the right to lay the rails across our land. I met with my attorney and the railroad men. It turns out that I got paid $1,000.00 for the right-of-way lease because the deal was made before Jud took the ranch from us. Grady, that $1,000.00 is all the money Marlene and I have in the world. So if I invest it with you can you promise me that you will do the things we have been talking about?"

"Oh no, I don't think I want that kind of responsibility on me."

"You want to go into business don't you?"

"Yes, but I couldn't live with myself if something went wrong. That is too scary Colleen."

"Look at it this way Grady. That $1,000.00 won't last us the rest of our lives that's for sure. I would go in business myself except in this day and time women don't do that. So you see we need you and you need us. Now I've been thinking Marlene and I can rent a room over at Mrs. Bradenton's boarding house for $8.00 a week. We can live there until the business can start paying us something to live on. If you are driving the wagon I can keep the books and write letters to potential new customers to help drum up more business."

"Have you already collected the money?"

"Yes, I got a bank draft for $1,000.00 this morning. How soon can you get a wagon and a team of draft mules?"

"They had a good wagon over at the wagon yard. In fact I put a deposit down on it before the fight. They were supposed to hold it for me until last Tuesday. I can run over there and see if it's still there. If it is we can get it today. There is a widow lady out east of town that has a good pair of draft mules we can get. The wagon cost $400.00 and she'll probably want $50.00 for the mules."

"Can you find a second pair of mules so you can do what you said about having a spare team tied to the back of the wagon?"

"What if that one is gone? How long will it take to get another one?"

"The wagon yard man said it would take three or four weeks to get another one."

"You run over there and see if the wagon is still there. I will go to Mr. Thacker's office and see if he has finished drawing up the partnership agreement."

Grady grabbed his hat and started for the door, then stopped and said, "Wait a minute. When did you tell him to draw up a partnership agreement?"

Colleen smiled and said, "This morning. I wasn't going to tell you until I was certain we could work together. Now partner get going and find us a wagon."

Grady shook he head and said, "I can see now this is going to be an exciting partnership with you two as my partners. Does Marlene even know about this?"

"Not yet."

CHAPTER TWENTY-NINE

J ud sat on his horse on the side of the hill watching the boys
bunch the herd below. *'Two thousand head makes quite a herd. I'm
glad I decided to increase it, two thousand is better than one thousand.
Just think it'll take them about ten or twelve days to reach the Fort Worth
stockyards. By the time the boys start back the railroad will be almost here
if not all the way here. They can ride the rails back so they can get here in
one day. I'll collect between $30,000.00 and $40,000.00, I'll be the richest
man in the territory.*

*When I get that money in my hands there ain't nobody that can stop me
then. Not that tin star sheriff, or that mouse of a marshal. In fact I may put
up one of my gunmen to run for sheriff in the next election. Then I'll really
own this territory.* He chuckled, "Hell there won't be anybody left to
vote against him."

Temple had been appointed trail boss for the drive, he lifted his hat and waved it forward. The cowboys started moving
the herd east. They didn't rush them--- they simply crowded the
herd and it moved away from them. In a little while the cattle

were strung out in a ragged line stretching a mile from end to end.

The marshal sat thinking about the murder, going over in his mind what he had done and what they had learned. He turned to one of his deputies and said, "It just occurred to me, we never did interview any of the people working in the saloon that night. I don't know what they could have seen or heard but that is a stone left unturned."

The deputy grabbed his hat and said, "Let's go before they get busy."

When they walked in the bartender said, "Come on in. It's pretty early for you boys, what'll you have?"

"Conn, we are here on official business. We need to ask you and your staff some questions about the night Mr. O'Shanity was murdered."

"That was about the worst thing I ever heard of. Killing an old man who was already paralyzed in his bed. What can we do to help you?"

"Do you remember who was in here that night?"

"No, marshal, there are so many people in here all the time, it's hard to remember a particular person on a particular night. I'm sorry."

"Do you remember if Jud Rawlins was in here that night?"

"Now that I do remember, because he was pretty drunk and beat up one of my girls pretty bad."

"Is she here now?"

"No she ain't come back to work yet, he left her face pretty bruised up."

"Y'all should have come and got me I'd have thrown him in jail that night."

"Now marshal you know how these gals are, if they come and got the law ever time some dude got drunk and a little rough with 'em pretty soon they wouldn't have any customers after word got around."

"Conn, this is a disgusting business you are in. Who else was working that night?"

"I guess everybody."

"Okay, we are gonna sit over at that table in the corner, one by one I want to talk to anybody and everybody who was working that night."

"Okay you want some coffee."

"Yeah, that would be good."

Over the next hour they talked to every person who worked that night, everybody remembered that Jud was there and that he was drunk. They especially remember how he punched Lizzie in the face for no reason. At the end of an hour the marshal turned to the deputy and said, "I haven't heard anything that would gave Jud a motive to kill Mr. O'Shanity. Other than the fact he is mean and he was drunk. Have you?"

"No, they say he didn't leave here until three or four in the morning and he was drunk. You don't suppose that he was mad drunk and just decided to go over there and kill the old man do you?"

"It is possible but we don't have anything to tie him to the killing, at least no motive."

"Other than the fact he is mean and he was drunk."

"Let's go find that dude and bring him in for questioning. He might slip up and say something that will give us a motive."

CHAPTER THIRTY

Grady hurried back to the lawyer's office and stepped through the door, "Good morning sir. You must be Grady?"

Grady stepped up and shook the hand that was offered.

Colleen said, "What did you find out?"

"It's there. But we have to hurry because a rancher is due in today to buy it. If he gets there first, we'll have to wait three of four weeks for him to get another one built and delivered."

"Mr. Thacker, can we take care of securing the wagon and then come back and sign the papers?'

"Colleen since you are my client, I will feel better if you will go to the bank and get the funds you need while Grady and I go over the paper work. I am sure that Grady is an honest business partner but as your attorney I want to get his signature on these documents before you hand over any money."

Colleen grabbed up her purse and said, "Okay Grady you sign the papers while I walk over to the bank and as soon as I get back we'll go straight to the wagon yard." She hurried out the door.

Marlene said, "Mrs. Sullivan do you know what's going on. Colleen has been acting funny the last couple of days?"

"No dear, in fact a couple of days ago Colleen said you were acting funny. Are you both hiding something from the other?"

"Do you remember when the pastor preached that sermon about giving up your life for someone else?"

"Yes that is a noble Christian virtue."

"Jud Rawlins has asked me to marry him."

"Oh dear, do you love him?"

"No in fact I can't stand him, but it would give Colleen and me some security."

"Is that what you meant by giving up your life for someone else?"

"Yes."

"That is a very noble thought on your part, but I suggest you sit down and talk to Colleen before you say yes. She may have some ideas of her own. It seems to me you had kind of a fondness for that young man Grady."

"Oh I do like Grady. I thought I would die when he was getting beat up so bad in the awful fight."

Mrs. Sullivan smiled and said, "Don't do anything until you two sisters have a chance to sit down and talk."

⊱✦⊰

The two marshal's met Jud on the street in front of the saloon. "Jud we are investigating the murder of Mr. O'Shanity. I want you to walk over to my office with us and answer some questions for me."

"Are you accusing me of murdering that old man?"

"We are not accusing you of anything yet. We just need for you to answer some questions. You can come voluntarily or we can put you in irons and take you."

"I don't know nothing about it so let's get this over with as you know I'm a busy man."

When they got in the office the marshal said, "Jud have a seat, do you want some coffee?"

"Hell no, this ain't no social call, you drug me in here so let's get on with it. I've got a lot more important things to do."

"You know when Mr. O'Shanity was murdered."

"Certainly everybody in town knows that."

"Where were you that night?"

"I was in the saloon all evening. You can ask anybody who works there, they'll tell you."

"Should we ask Lizzie?"

Jud shot up out of his chair, "Is that little whore trying to press charges against me?"

"Sit down Jud. No Lizzie is not pressing charges against you. I wish she would, I'd throw you in the cell and keep you there until the circuit judge comes through here and I'd see that he didn't come very soon."

Jud eased back into is chair.

"I told you we are trying to find the person who murdered Mr. O'Shanity. Do you know of anybody who would want to kill that old man?"

"No I don't. It is a fact that I held a note on his ranch and I now own it but I offered to let him live there. I even offered him $500.00 walking around money."

"The only way he could get that is if his daughter married you, is that right?"

"No, I did ask his daughter to marry me and I didn't want my father-in-law to be walking around penniless."

"What do you know about the Worthington killing?"

"That is not in your jurisdiction. I've already talked to the sheriff about that. Do you have anything else you want to ask me about Mr. O'Shanity?"

CHAPTER THIRTY-ONE

Temple rode up to the chuck wagon and tied his horse to the wagon tongue. Pouring himself some strong black coffee he said, "I don't like the looks of them clouds coming in from the North West."

The cook looked at them and said, "They are pretty black, but they're still a good ways off. Maybe they'll pass north of us."

"I hope so. I don't like nurse maidin' these stupid beefs no way and I sure don't want to do it during no down pour."

"I got a pot of beans with some ham hock in 'em and some cornbread in the Dutch oven, help yourself."

"Did you see them injunes shadowing us all day? Better double the night guard. They may try to sneak in and steal some beef or some horses."

Soon they were all gathered around the black iron pot except two left out with the herd.

While they were eating Temple spoke up and said, "Boys tonight we are going to keep three men on watch instead of two."

"Awe man what are you thinkin'? We won't get as much sleep that way."

"Look over toward the sunset. See them black clouds gathering up. We may get hit with a storm before morning so be sure to take your rain slicker with ya. That ain't all, me and cookie have both been seein' Injunes following us all day. They may try to sneak in here tonight and steal some beef or some horses."

"Hell I say we just give 'em all they want, after all they 're stolen cows any way."

"Boys we was hired to do a job, now like it or not we are gonna do it. It ain't none of my business where the man got them cow critters, all I know is he is paying me good wages to get 'em to Fort Worth. I ride for the brand and in this case that means I ride for the man who's paying the wages. You three," pointing to three sitting on the right side of the fire, "you go out there and relieve them two so they can come in and get some vitals. The rest of you turn in."

"Little John, you and Turley and Jake take the next shift. Walker, you and Rod and Curley take the midnight. Me and the other two will take the 3:00 shift."

When the three riders came out from camp, one of the guys who had stayed with the herd said, "Fellows I don't know what's goin' on but somethin' is spookin' these critters. You watch 'em you'll see what I mean."

A deputy sheriff walked in and said, "Another barn burned down last night."

"Whose?"

"That sod buster out by Pecan Gap."

"I wonder how they are starting the fires"

"I know how they started this one."

"How?"

"They used a can of coal-oil."

"What's that?"

"Some call it Kerosene, the old timers call it coal oil."

"How do you know that is what they used?"

"Because the sod buster heard 'em prowling around and when the fire started he took a shot at 'em, they took off and left a bucket behind half full of coal-oil."

"Starting tonight, I want all of you working the night shift. I want you to go out in twos and cover as much of the county as you can. Maybe we'll get lucky and catch us a couple of high binders with a can of coal-oil."

"You know Jud is puttin' pressure on the Birchfield's to sell out now. So far he hasn't done anything but hint to them bad things could happen to them if they don't sign over their title at his ridiculous low price."

"Maybe I'll get lucky and he'll try to pull a gun on me."

CHAPTER THIRTY-TWO

Colleen and Grady walked to the wagon yard, there sat a shiny green freight wagon with high side boards and big wide wheels. It looked strong enough to haul any load.

Grady ran his hand down the side of the wagon and said, "Isn't she a thing of beauty?"

Colleen laughed and said, "Grady I have never thought of a freight wagon as a thing of beauty. Now that you mention it, it is kind-ah pretty in it's own special way."

"Come on let's go see the man and just hope we are in time."

The two railroad agents walked back into the lawyer's office. "You sent a message you wanted to see us. I hope there is nothing wrong with the lease."

"Oh, no, there is nothing wrong with your lease. It is already filed at the county seat. I have something else that might interest you gentlemen."

"Your rail will be here in this area or I should say passing through this area soon."

"Yes now that all of the leases are signed it is coming right on through."

"Then let me speculate as to why you are still here.

Both agents looked at each other, "Okay."

"You need a shipping and a passenger depot. I have a suggestion for you to consider."

⇥ ⇤

Jud pulled up in front of the pastor's house in a sparkling new buckboard pulled by a team of sleek black horses. When Mrs. Sullivan opened the door he politely removed his hat, and with a slight bow said, "Good morning Mrs. Sullivan. I would like to speak to Miss Marlene."

"Good morning Mr. Rawlins. Is she expecting you?"

"No ma'am, I thought I would surprise her with a picnic on a beautiful day like today."

"Without a chaperone?"

"My dear lady it is broad day light and Miss Marlene is over eighteen years old. Surely she can go without a chaperone, if she wants."

Marlene appeared at the door, "Jud, I wasn't expecting you. Come in."

"My dear it is a beautiful day and I wanted to surprise you with a picnic. I have a carriage and lunch is packed for us. Shall we go?"

"Oh my, what a surprise. Let me get my bonnet."

Jud tipped his hat to Mrs. Sullivan and took Marleen's elbow and escorted her to the waiting carriage. In a very gentleman way he assisted her into the carriage. Jud walked around the carriage and lifted a lap robe from behind the seat and spread it across Marleen's lap.

"We don't want to get your beautiful gown dusty."

"Oh Jud, this old thing is not a beautiful gown. This is a house dress. I wasn't expecting to meet a gentleman today."

"On you my darling everything looks like a beautiful gown."

It was a perfect day for a picnic, it had rained during the night, the air was crisp and clean. As they rode along the lane they came upon a young farmer and his wife who had a problem. His wagon wheels on the right side had gotten off the road and was stuck in the soft wet ground beside the hard packed road. The man was straining to push the wagon while the young wife was trying to drive the team.

"Oh Jud can't we help them?"

Jud shot her an annoyed look then caught himself and said, "Certainly dearest, I was just going to suggest that myself."

Jud stopped the buggy and unhooked his team of horses and moved them over to the wagon and hooked them up with the mules pulling the wagon and the four animals had no trouble moving the wagon back on to the hard ground.

The young farmer said, "Sir I sure do thank you. I would offer to pay except we have no cash money. My Missy has put up some fine fig preserves let me give you a couple of jars." He reached into the back of the wagon and pulled out two fruit jars full of fig preserves.

"Oh no sir, you keep 'em we are going on a picnic, and happy to help. You can pay me back by helping the next person you see stuck by the side of a road."

The young farmer stuck out his hand and shook Jud's hand, that is kindly of you sir. I sure will."

When Jud got back in the buggy Marlene said, "That was sweet of you."

Soon Jud wheeled the buggy up in the shade of two giant oak trees on a bluff overlooking the river. The view was magnificent.

As he spread a quilt on the ground and opened a picnic basket. He said, "Tell me about school. Surly a sophisticated lady like your self is ready to be finished with children's games."

"I wouldn't call finishing school, children's games. The studies are very hard."

"Please forgive me my darling, I never meant to belittle the effort you are putting in. It's just, well you seem so mature and you certainly are beautiful. What type of things are you learning?"

"Well we have classes on social graces. We have classes on the most modern dances. Each girl is required to master one musical instrument before she can graduate. She must be able to plan and prepare a banquet meal. She must know how to supervise a staff of domestic employees."

"Oh my dear Marleen, you are more perfect than I thought."

"What on earth do you mean Mr. Rawlins?"

"Please call me Jud. Let me explain, I'm going to be one of, if not the wealthiest man in this state. I shall even run for governor. To be the wife of the governor takes a special kind of lady. She must have your type of beauty. She must have all the social graces. It would be imperative that she know how to supervise a staff of domestic employees. If she could play a musical instrument that would be valuable in helping to entertain important guests. I can see your beauty, I never dreamed you would also have all of the other skills needed to be the first lady."

"Jud, I am only eighteen."

"My dear Marleen, how old was your mother when she married that fine man who became your father?"

"She was sixteen."

"Don't you see dear, you were her age two years ago? I'm so happy that you waited until now to choose me to be your husband. Let's race back to town and find the judge and get married today."

"Oh no Jud, you are very charming and handsome, but when I get married I want a wedding with flowers and music and bunting, I want it to be an occasion."

Jud took her hand and softly kissed it, "I am sorry my darling, I get so excited when I think about you being my wife, I can hardly contain myself. Please forgive me. I know it appears to be sudden but when destiny strikes, you must grab the moment before it slips away. "

"Jud, please take me back home. You make it sound so exciting you sweep a girl off her feet. I must have time to think and make plans."

"Oh my darling, I know it is enough to make a beautiful maiden's head spin, but if we race to town and grab a judge and get married I will take you on the most exquisite honeymoon and all the time we are visiting San Francisco, London, Paris and the orient, you can be planning that new home I am going to have built just for you my bride. Won't all those girls from your school be jealous with envy when they hear about your station in life?"

Oh crap, I pushed too fast. I don't want to lose this little Pidgeon. "Of course my darling. It is just that things are moving so fast in this time period, we want to ride the crest of the wave. I am so taken by your beauty I can hardly sleep at night. Marleen I love you."

When they arrived back at the Sullivan's Jud like a gentleman helped Marleen down from the buggy and escorted her to the door step. He gently lifted her hand and kissed it saying, "jusqu'à demain." He tipped his hat and walked back to the carriage.

Mrs. Sullivan opened the door, "I trust your picnic was enjoyable."

"Oh Mrs. Sullivan it was magical. Did you hear what he said just now?"

"I wasn't eavesdropping but the front door was open and I could hear through the screen door."

"What was it he said when he kissed my hand? It sounded French."

"It was French and it meant, until tomorrow."

"That is the problem. He was a perfect gentleman and he is very handsome, he is also in a very big hurry."

"What do you mean Marleen?"

"He wanted me to race back to town and go find a judge and get married this afternoon."

"Today?"

"Yes."

"You hardly know the man. I don't remember ever seeing him at church services."

"Oh but he makes it sound so exciting. He wants to become the governor and make me the first lady. Entertain important guests at lavish parties."

"Marleen, fast talking men have been talking young women into doing things they later regret ever since that smooth talking devil talked Eve into eating that apple in the garden of Eden. My only advice is take it slow, don't let Jud Rawlins stampede you into doing something that you will regret the rest of your life. If he is sincere, he can wait and give you time to make plans and make certain that this is what you really want. Think hard about what you really want, because it does sound like he'll be back tomorrow."

The marshal walked back into the saloon and said, "Is Lizzie back to work?"

"Yes, she is."

In a few minutes a diminutive young woman appeared from the back room, "You want to see me marshal?"

"Yes Lizzie, can we sit down and talk for a minute?"

"Sure we don't have any customers right now anyway."

"Lizzie, I heard about what happened to you. If anything like that ever happens again, I want you to come and tell me. I will throw him under the jail."

She gave a little giggle and said, "I would like to see that. How you would pick up the jail and throw somebody under it."

"Lizzie it's just an old saying. If you tell me the next time someone beats you up I will throw him in the jail and keep him there for a long time. Now let me ask you about something else. On the night, Jud beat you up, did you see or hear anything out of the ordinary before he beat you up."

"No. He was drinking a lot but he always does."

"What set him off? Why did he start beating you?"

"I don't know. Wait a minute, now I remember it was right after he heard those two railroad men talking about making a deal with Mr. O'Shanity."

"Whoa, what did you just say?"

"You know those walls in the saloon are real thin, so you can hear people talking sometimes. These two railroad men were talking about making a deal with Mr. O'Shanity and they were going to go back in the morning and pay him some money. I was trying to tell Jud something and he told me to shut up, he wanted to hear what they were saying."

"Then what happened?"

"He was sittin' on the bed with his ear to the wall. Then he jumped up and started pacing the floor cussin' a blue streak. I went over to him and told him to calm down. That's when he jumped on me."

"Could you hear what the men said, or is that what Jud said, they said?"

"I couldn't hear every word like he could because he had his ear up against the wall. I just heard them say 'I'm glad we went to see O'Shanity directly and made a deal.'"

"Lizzie that is important. I want you to walk over to my office and write down what you just told me and sign it."

"I'm not in trouble am I?"

"No darlin', you definitely are not."

CHAPTER THIRTY-THREE

One of the men from the midnight crew came in and woke Temple and his men. "Temple you guys are probably gonna get wet. There ain't a star in the sky and it is black as a dungeon out there. Them cow critters is skittish as a bunch of old maids at a fiddlers contest."

Riding out Temple said, "Boys you better keep singing as you ride around so you don't startle any of them and start a stampede."

"Temple I feel the hair on the back of my neck standing up. Something weird is going on. I don't like any of this."

It was hard to tell time without seeing the stars. Temple could tell the herd was growing more restless every time he made the circle. The cattle were up on their feet, he could hear horns clashing, steers bawling. Over all the pandemonium he heard the other two riders singing as loud as they could to try and calm everything down.

Suddenly a blue green light danced across the horns of a hundred steers. Then a blinding flash. Temple was knocked from his horse by the concussion of a blast. Then two thousand 1200 pound steers were in full flight scattering in every direction.

Several of the punchers were still in their bedrolls asleep when a thundering herd crashed through camp.

The sun was barely up, Colleen was waiting at the wagon yard, when Grady came back to town leading a team of draft mules. "My goodness Grady they are big."

"They need to be to pull that wagon when it's loaded down. Let me get them in harness and drive the freighter over to the feed mill. I'll get'er loaded and we'll make our first haul today."

"Where is our first load going?"

"A big dairy farm about fifteen miles east."

"How much is this load gonna pay?"

"$60.00."

"I'll go to the bank and get us an account open. Mr. Thacker sent word he wanted to see one of us today Do you know what he wants?"

"No but it's too late for the railroad to get their money back. It's gone."

"Have we got a load for tomorrow?"

"Yep, We've got a load of feed going to Cisco and then I've got to drive another fifteen miles and pick up a load of iron ingots for the blacksmith so we'll get paid twice tomorrow."

"Do you mean we could make $100.00 in one day?"

"A little more because I get paid $60.00 for one and $50.00 for the other."

"We need to find that spare team right away."

"I heard there's a guy out at Buffalo Gap that's got a team of greys. Sunday I'll ride out and check on'em."

The sun was just peeping over the ridge in the east when Grady was hitching up the team. He turned and said, "Come on Knot let's go haul some freight."

Knot got a running start and bounded up on the seat.

Grady climbed up and said, "Scoot over you big lug, leave room for me unless you plan on driving."

Knot's tail thumped the wooden seat.

The sun was sitting in the west when Grady unhooked his team. The holster (man who handles horses) came out and said, "Miss Colleen wants you to come over to the parson's house as soon as you get here. She said she had something important to talk to you about."

When Grady got to the Sullivan's house Knot curled up at the foot of the steps. Grady stepped up on the porch and saw Mrs. Sullivan was sitting in the parlor knitting. The wood door was open so he spoke through the screen door, "Good evening ma'am I didn't want to startle you. Colleen sent word for me to come over as soon as I got back to town."

"Oh hello Mr. McCain."

She wrinkled her nose and said, "To tell you the truth, after the fight got started I found myself hoping you'd win even though I'd bet on the other guy."

Grady laughed and said, "Well ma'am that's comforting."

Colleen heard Grady talking and came into the room, "Oh good, you made it back. Did everything go alright?"

"Yes, just a long hard drive, but a profitable day."

"Come in the kitchen, I'll make some coffee. Mrs. Sullivan, would you like some?"

"No dear if I drink any this late I won't sleep a wink all night. You two go ahead. You've got business to talk about."

Colleen looked at Grady and thought, *he looks dead tired, I picked a great partner.* Marlene needs to grab this boy or man.

"We need to get another wagon."

Grady laughed, "Whoa Colleen, we've only been in business two days and we've only taken in $170.00. That ain't enough to buy another wagon yet. How about we get you and Marlene out of the preacher's house before we start expanding the business."

"Here is your coffee. You need to be awake when I tell you what I did today while you were gone."

"Oh Colleen that scares me. What did you do?"

"Remember I told you Mr. Thacker wanted to see one of us. That one was me. When I got there the two railroad agents were there. Mr. Thacker is drawing up a contract for us to have the exclusive right to haul all the freight from the train depot to the customers within a fifty mile distance."

"Wow, Colleen that's great. When're we supposed to sign it?"

"It will be ready to sign in the morning. Unless you want to sign it, I will go ahead and sign for both of us."

"Heck no lady you're on a roll. I'll go drive the wagon, you make the deals. How soon before the railroad expects to have a stop here?"

"About three weeks."

"Why don't you go over to the wagon yard in the morning after you sign the contract and put $100.00 down on a new wagon and get him to order it? Tell him to put a rush on it. Maybe we can get it here by the time they are ready to have freight for us to haul."

"Grady I've still got $400.00 left out of that $1,000.00 they paid me. I could go ahead and buy the wagon now and the company could reimburse me."

"No Colleen, the company can pay him $100.00 now and we'll have the money to pay all of it when the wagon gets here."

That's assuming nothing goes wrong.

CHAPTER THIRTY-FOUR

When Lizzie finished writing out everything she had told the marshal he had her sign it in front of a Notary.

When she had gone, the marshal said, "Okay fellows we now have a motive. I want to put the cuffs on that arrogant joker."

"You want us to go pick him up?"

"Not yet. Just having a motive to commit a crime is not proof he did it. Go find me something that will hang that dude. If he really did it?"

"Have you ever figured out how that little gold chain link fits in?"

The sheriff's nightriders didn't catch anybody with a can of coal-oil but they did catch three of Jud's men rustling Box M cattle.

"Okay boy's you know cattle rustling can be a hanging offense. It's up to the judge. All I want to know is who told you to go steal those cows? You give me his name and I'll talk to the judge."

"Ain't nobody told us nothin' we just needed a little drinkin' money so we rounded up a few steers that was runnin' loose out there and was drivin' em' in to get some drinkin' money. Ain't hardly a puncher on the range that ain't rounded up a few strays for drinkin' money from time to time. Ain't no judge gonna hang a man for that."

"Yes, well you had one hundred and fifty head when you were caught. That is a lot more than a couple head for drinkin' money."

⊷⊹ ⊹⊷

"Marleen, please sit down we need to talk."

"Okay what do you want to talk about?"

"I understand Jud took you on a picnic today."

"Yes he did."

"What happened?"

"First of all big sister, I am eighteen, I do not need your permission to go on a picnic. Second he was a perfect gentleman. He asked me to marry him."

"What did you tell him?"

"I told him he made it sound very exciting, but I needed time to think."

"Marleen, you can't seriously think about marrying that man."

"Why not, what other options do we have? He owns our home, we have no money, he is very handsome and he is a gentleman."

"Marleen think about what you are saying, he is no gentleman. He tried to force me to marry him and when I refused he started on you."

"So this is about the fact you're jealous of your little sister."

"No Marleen, I told him in no uncertain terms that I was not interested in him now or ever. "

"So, you are not jealous? What about the fact we are penniless and homeless? He said if I married him, I would have a home and we would see that you were taken care of."

"Well first of all we are no longer penniless. It turns out the railroad made a deal with daddy to lease the right of way to lay tracks across our land."

"We don't own the land anymore."

"That is right but the deal with daddy was made before some low life sneaked in through the window and murdered him. I think the murderer is Jud Rawlins."

"I asked Jud about that and he told me he didn't do it and he had no reason to do it because he already had the ranch."

"He didn't already have the ranch when the deal was done. That is why the rail road paid me as executor of daddy's estate a check for $1,000.00 so we are no longer penniless."

"When did you find all this out?"

"Yesterday while you were on a picnic with Mr. Jud Rawlins. That is not all, I invested half the money into a freight hauling business with Grady. He and I have purchased a freight wagon. He is going to drive it and deliver freight, we will get paid $60.00 a load. He thinks he can haul one load every day except Sunday, so the business will earn between $200.00 and $300.00 every week. He will get half the profit and we will get half."

"Does Jud know about this?"

"Yes the railroad men told him night before last."

"So all the time he was telling me all that stuff about taking care of us, he already knew about the check you were getting."

"Oh my-gosh Colleen, what a fool I've been.! I guess I am not as grown up as I thought. No wonder he tried so hard to get me to go find the judge and get married yesterday." She started to cry.

<hr>

The marshal walked into the jewelers, "Good morning Mr. Moskowitz." I'm still trying to find the chain this link came off of. Have you thought any more about it?"

"Well now that's a funny thing. I've got one right here that matches the link you found. It's a gold watch chain for a man's watch. Remember I said the link was too big for a ladies necklace. Look at this chain, it's the same as the one you have. A fellow brought it in and wanted me to mount a silver dollar on the end for a watch fob."

"Who does it belong to?

"Jud Rawlins, he used to have a big gold nugget on the chain but said he lost it so he wants me to put a shiny new silver dollar on it."

CHAPTER THIRTY-FIVE

Every morning Grady was up before dawn. Harnessed his team and climbed up on that hard wooden seat. He would drive to the feed mill, Ronnie and Lonnie would help him load two thousand pounds of feed into the wagon and he would be off.

Soon word spread that he was a dependable, sober teamster and he started getting more freight. Often he would haul feed out and return with a different commodity. Grady quickly went from earning $12.00 a week working at the feed mill to earning $300.00 a week delivering freight.

By the time he unharnessed the team every night he was so tired he didn't know he and Colleen were growing wealthy. Colleen on the other hand was adding up the deliveries and depositing the money in the bank. She couldn't believe what she was seeing. Every night she would read her columns. This is unbelievable. We have only been in business a little over a month and after paying for the feed and paying Mr. Bledsoe, we still have over $1,500.00 in the bank."

"Pardner unless something really bad happens we're on our way to having a thriving business." Grady said.

The marshal rode up to the sheriff's office and stepped down from the saddle.

Sheriff Adams saw him dismounting and said, "Well marshal what brings you over here?"

"Let's go inside and talk."

"You must have something important, come on in."

"We need to go pick up Jud Rawlins."

"There ain't nothing I'd like better. What-cha got?"

The marshal told him about the written statement from Lizzie.

The sheriff said, "That's good but I don't think that's enough for us to charge him with murder."

"That's not all. Remember the link off a gold chain I found outside the window the killer climbed through."

"Yes."

"I went back to the jeweler, it just so happens that he has a gold watch chain that Jud had brought in to have repaired and the link matches. It seems that Jud had a gold watch chain with a large gold nugget attached. He lost the gold nugget somewhere and brought the chain in for the jeweler to attach a shiny new silver dollar in its place."

"Whew, I like that. Before we go pick him up maybe you should look one more time and see if you can find that gold nugget. If you find that nugget then we can slam the door on him for good."

"I got real excited when I found that chain. I'll bet you're right. He can claim he lost it out hunting or something. Dog gone-it, I want to catch that dude so bad I can taste it."

"You and me both. I have all my deputies riding night watch right now. Because of all them barn fires. We found out they were using coal-oil to set the barns on fire. We have been riding all night hoping to catch some dude with a can of fuel. So far we haven't caught anybody carrying coal-oil but we did catch three of Jud's men rustling Box M cattle. I've got them here in jail."

"He's getting short on man power then."

"Yeah, he sent nine on a trail drive to Fort Worth. I wish I could have seen the brands on that herd before it left the county."

"Do you sometimes feel our hands are tied behind our back, while the law protects the bad guys?"

"Marshal I know exactly how you feel, but you know as well as I do that if we don't do everything by the law book, a judge will turn them loose every time. I sure don't want to arrest him and have some judge turn him loose. When I think of that young widow and those youngens, I want to see him hang."

"Every time I think of that nice old man lying in bed paralyzed, and some low life crawling in a window and smothering him to death with a pillow, cause he couldn't fight back. I just want to scream I am so mad."

—◄+►—

Jud was pacing the floor in the ranch house, grumbling. "Of all the rotten luck. The boys getting caught with that bunch of Box M cattle. Who would have thought a bunch of deputy sheriffs would be out riding around in the middle of the night. Well at least Temple and the guys should reach Fort Worth next week. Then I'll show these hay seeds a thing or two."

One of the men sitting on the porch said, "Riders coming."

Jud walked to the door to see who was coming. "It looks like a couple of the riders from the trail drive. They couldn't be all the way to Fort Worth yet, could they?"

They stood there watching as two horses trotted into the yard and two riders covered in trail dust dismounted, whipping dust off their chaps with their hats.

"What the hell are you two doing back here, where are the rest of 'em and where is my money?"

"There ain't no more and there ain't no money."

"Huh, what did you say? Where is my herd?"

"Lightning struck the herd and killed a couple of hundred steers, and the rest of 'em stampeded in every direction."

"How come you're the only ones to come back? Are the rest of 'em out there trying to round up my herd? Why ain't cha out there with 'em?"

"No they're all dead."

Shaking his head in disbelief Jud said, "Man you ain't makin' no sense, what do you mean they're all dead?"

"I saw the lightening knock Temple off his horse, the rest of 'em were in their bedrolls when the herd stampeded right over 'em. The only reason we're here's because we were on the side away from the direction the main herd went. Instead of running over us they ran away from us."

Jud took a step back and sat down on the front step of the house, and buried his face in his hands. "Leave me alone, I've gotta think a minute."

One of the riders looked around, "Where's everybody else?"

"Well if you remember there wasn't but five of us left here, three of 'em got caught rustlin' a herd of Box M cattle and they're sitting in the jail waiting for the judge to get here."

"Does that mean we're through?'

"No, you know Jud, he'll think of something."

"I hope he does cause I'm flat broke. I ain't even got enough to buy a sack of smoking tobacco."

CHAPTER THIRTY-SIX

Three weeks later, the new wagon arrived. Grady had bought the other pair of gray draft mules. He and his wagons were ready when the first train stopped at a make shift loading dock they had hastily assembled. Grady shook hands with the conductor who handed him a hand full of bill-of-ladings. Then he handed him a clip board with a copy of each bill-of-lading on it.

"Sir if you will just sign each of these forms we will officially transfer all of this freight to you."

As the train pulled out Grady turned to Ronnie and Lonnie and said, "Okay boys welcome to the freight business. Lonnie pull your wagon up first and we'll get you loaded, since your run is the longest. Then we'll get Ronnie loaded up. Don't forget to collect the money for the freight from each delivery or you'll have a red-head Irish lady down on you quick."

"We ain't scared of you but we sure don't want Miss Colleen on us." Both guys were grinning as they walked to their wagons.

"Ronnie as soon as you drop off that load over at the mercantile, come back to the feed mill and get that load for the Circle S."

Late that evening as both wagons were parked and the mules bedded down in the livery, Grady, Lonnie and Ronnie were walking across the street to get a bite to eat at Mays. Ronnie was carrying a Winchester rifle and Lonnie had a 12-gauge scatter gun. They heard the sound of horses racing down the street, people were running in both directions to get out of the way.

The three of them were caught in the middle of the road as Jud and four remaining gunmen thundered toward them. One of the gunman reached down and tried to part Grady's hair with the barrel of a six-shooter saying, "Get out of the way."

Grady grabbed the hand holding the six-shooter and the momentum of the running horse jerked the rider right over the horse's rump. He sat down hard in the middle of the street. The others reined their mounts around ready to enjoy the show. When the gunman leaped up off the ground Grady was still holding the man's six-shooter in his hand. He tried to bend the steel barrel over the man's head.

Jud started to reach for his gun, then everybody along Main Street heard the unmistakable sound of two hammers being cocked back. "I'm bettin' this scatter gun can clear three of you right out of the saddle with one blast. Ronnie can you and Grady handle the rest?"

Jud was fighting mad but only a fool would argue with a 12 gauge shotgun and a Winchester at this range. We was just coming in to have a drink. We don't want no trouble. No hard feelings."

Grady said, "You know what boys I believe these fellows was just being a little unruly, they say they didn't mean no hard feeling. I'll believe them completely when they drop them gun belts down in the street. Unbuckle 'em real easy and let 'em drop right down in the street."

One of the hired guns swore and said, "The devil himself couldn't get me to drop my gun in the street."

Grady's forty-four appeared in his hand and the man's hat flew off his head along with a large chunk of his left ear. "If you don't get that gun belt off right now you and the devil will be discussing it in less than a minute."

Nobody had ever seen gun belts shed so fast.

"Boys your gun belts will be waiting for you at the marshal's office in the morning. Now y'all have a good night."

When they got through eating Grady looked at the list of incoming freight the conductor had left with him and thought. *Oh my goodness, we need another wagon right now.*

Marlene and Colleen had moved into Mrs. Bradenton's rooming house, she had allowed them to set up a freight office in Colleen's room.

Knot took up the sentry position by the front steps. Grady tapped on the door.

Mrs. Bradenton looked up and saw it was Grady said, "Come on in Mr. McCain."

Colleen came into the kitchen, "Well did we get a lot of freight?"

"We did." He handed her the bill-of-ladings that he had sent out with Lonnie and Ronnie. Then he said, "We've got a problem."

Colleen said, "We have more than one problem. Tell me yours first."

"We need another wagon right now. Look at what is due in here in the next five days." He handed her the list the conductor had given him. "Mr. Johnson tells me he's going to have a lot of feed for us to deliver too."

"What was your news?"

"First let me ask you a question. Do you really like Marlene?"

"Please don't take offense at this but I think Marlene is the most beautiful girl or woman I have ever seen in my life." Grady said, "She is also smart, witty, caring. Do you remember the way she cared for that little bird that broke his wing. She babied it until it could fly again on its own. Do I like her? I think I love her.

When we get the business more stabilized. I plan on courting her properly. Its kind-a funny since your dad's gone, I guess I need to get your permission."

"Grady that's what I wanted to talk to you about. Jud's really putting the rush on Marlene trying to get her to agree to marry him. She has told him no, but he is very pushy and he can be pretty persuasive."

"He's too old for her. Didn't he try the same thing with you?"

"Yes, he did. I turned him down and he didn't want to take no for my answer. He was so pushy my daddy told him to wait until he could go get his gun on and they would step out in the front yard and settle this matter once and for all. Marleen is young, and she has a very sensitive heart. I don't know what lies he is feeding her. She cannot marry that man. I still believe he killed my daddy. If I could prove it I would shoot him myself."

"Colleen that would be horrible. What can I do to stop it from happening?"

"Grady, I know she likes you, a lot, in fact she even commented that you were the man she was going to marry. Before Jud started moving in on her. Did you know, he came and got her the other day and took her on a picnic all alone."

"Maybe I will go shoot him," Grady said.

"You said, you guessed, you would need to ask my permission before you started courting my sister. Well partner you've got it. Now go over to the mercantile and get you a new set of courting clothes and get started courting my little sister."

The marshal, the sheriff and four deputies showed up at Hill-Valley ranch. The sheriff turned to the deputies and said, "You guys keep your eye on this bunch out here. Me and the marshal are going in to get Jud Rawlins."

The marshal knocked on the door. Jud opened the door. He was facing two drawn guns. "What is this all about?"

"We're taking you in."

"What for?"

"You got some questions to answer about the killing of Mr. O'Shanity."

"I told you I don't know nothing about that old man getting killed."

"Let's go get your horse and we'll talk about it after we get to the sheriff's office. Come on," the marshal said.

They didn't tie his hands, but they did make sure he wasn't packing a gun. Twenty minutes later Jud rode up in front of the sheriff's office surrounded by six armed men.

The marshal and the sheriff walked in with Jud. The sheriff indicated a chair in front of his desk and said, "Okay Jud tell us again what you know about Mr. O'Shanity's killing."

"I told you clowns before, I don't know nothing about no killing of that old man or anybody else."

The sheriff said, "Jud I'm going to give you one more chance to save a hanging. Because if they find you guilty of smothering that old man in his bed with a canvas pillow they're going to march you right out and hang you. You know how western men are about murdering a defenseless old man in his bed. You can come clean right now and we'll talk to the judge and he'll send you to Parchman Prison, which is a lot better than the hanging tree."

"I told you I don't know nothing about that old man getting killed. I want to get my lawyer in here."

"You'll get a chance to talk to a lawyer later. Right know let me tell you what we know and let's see how you feel about talking to us after you see what we already know." The sheriff indicated that the marshal should talk next.

"Mr. Rawlings, there was one thing that's always bothered us. It was the fact we could not see why you would have a motive to kill

Mr. O'Shanity. You already had his ranch or at least a note on his ranch. You were already courting his daughter. So the question we kept asking ourselves was why?"

"We have talked to Lizzie and now we have a motive. Here is what we know."

"You heard the railroad men talking in the saloon about making a deal with Mr. O'Shanity. So you went over and murdered him in his bed, then jumped up and sent a telegram to an attorney to execute the claim on the note early the next morning. So you could collect the money from the railroad."

"We also know you climbed through the window and killed Mr. O'Shanity because that gold chain you used to wear is now over at Mr. Morawitz getting a silver dollar hung on the end of it because you broke it when you climbed through the window. We know this because we found a gold link off your chain in the dust below the window."

The sheriff looked Jud right in the eye and said, "Now. What have you got to say?"

CHAPTER THIRTY-SEVEN

Colleen walked into Mr. Thacker's office and said "Good morning sir."

"Hello Colleen, top of the morning to ya. Do you drink coffee?"

"Every now and then."

"I have some fresh if you would like a cup."

"Not today thank you."

"The railroad men will be here in just a moment they want to talk to you."

"Are they not happy with the service we are giving them?"

"I'll let them explain it to you when they get here."

⇒⟨⟩⟨⟩⟨⟩⇐

In the meantime Grady was riding on the seat with Ronnie on their way back to the train depot with a load of furs they had picked up at the tanner's. When they rounded a bend, the road was blocked by two men on horses wearing bandanas over their faces.

The masked man on the right said, "Climb down off that wagon we're taking the wagon and the load. At least it ain't far, you can walk back to town."

Grady said under his breath, "You take the one on the left."

Grady turned like he was getting ready to climb down. The gunman was shocked when a blazing forty four six-shooter appeared in Grady's hand."

The second would be gunman was just as surprised when he looked and realized he was looking down the barrel of a forty-four that Ronnie was holding in his hand.

The man slowly raised his hands.

Grady said, "Mister unless you want the same thing your buddy got you get that bandana off your face so I can see who you are."

The guy slowly reached up and pulled the bandana off his face.

"Now I know what you look like don't let me ever see you around one of my wagons again. I'll blast you right out of the saddle if you come within fifty yards of one of my wagons. Now get down and pick up that trash out of the road and get out of here before I change my mind and let Ronnie shoot you right now. He hadn't shot nobody yet this week. Furthermore you tell Jud that if anybody bothers another one of my wagons I'll come after him."

CHAPTER THIRTY-EIGHT

Grady stopped by the mercantile and purchased a new pair of black corduroy pants, a new white shirt with pearl buttons and a brand new pair of boots. Then he went back and got a blue scarf with gold thread around the hem and tied it around his neck. Then he and Knot went to the creek so he could take a bath.

After he got all dressed up he said, "Well Knot, how do you think I look?"

The dog rolled its head to one side and looked at him.

"Well what do you know, you're just a dog. Come on let's go a courtin'."

Grady tapped on the door frame. Mrs. Bradenton came to the door, "good evening Mr. McCain, I almost didn't recognize you. Do you wish to see Miss Colleen?"

"No ma'am, I would like to see Miss Marlene."

Grady had stopped and picked a hand full of wild flowers on the way back from the creek. In the middle of the bunch he had several sprigs of honey suckle, which really smelled good.

"Oh that's who the flowers are for, just a minute." She disappeared back in the house.

After minutes later Marleen walked up to the door. "You wanted to see me?"

Grady handed her the flowers.

"Oh thank you." She smelled of the bouquet and smiled, "I think this is the first time a gentleman has brought me flowers."

"Marleen can we sit here on the porch and visit a few minutes?"

"Well Mr. McCain it is a beautiful evening, I would be delighted to sit and visit with you. Is this an official courting visit?"

Grady could feel the heat rising in his neck and face. "Ah, yes, yes it is."

"Well I am flattered, that a handsome cowboy dressed as you are would like to sit and visit. What shall we talk about?"

Grady caught the twinkle in her eyes and said, "Well Miss Marleen O'Shanity, we could talk of many things. We could talk of the size of the moon, or the beauty of the light as it reflects off your beautiful red hair. Or we could talk of how beautiful your green eyes look. Then again we could just talk about how beautiful you are in total rather than in parts. I suspect you would rather talk about your school. So please tell me all about Boston and your school."

Marleen smiled and said, "Well done Mr. McCain, you skillfully changed the subject you started out with. However before we get to Boston, why don't you tell me why you agreed to get into that awful prize fight?"

"Did you enjoy watching the fight?"

"No, I never want to see another one, ever. I am surprised that you are okay now. I was scared you were going to be hurt badly."

"Believe me for a few days I did hurt badly, but so did Lonnie."

"Explain to me why you agreed to it."

"It was my idea."

"It was? Why on earth would you suggest something as grotesque as a prize fight?"

"I needed five hundred dollars to purchase a freight wagon. I couldn't think of any other way to raise five hundred dollars, so I thought we would stage a prize fight and sell tickets."

"I saw a lot of people there so you must have collected a lot of money."

"We did except Ronnie bet all of it on me since Jud was giving three to one odds."

She was silent for a few moment then said, "Do you mean you got all beat up for nothing?"

"Yes, let's talk about something else. Tell me about your school."

All at once Jud appeared out of the darkness. "Get away from my girl."

"Jud Rawlins I am not, your girl. Why are you here, what do you want?"

"I came to see you. Now field hand you get lost. I don't want to ever see you here again."

Grady slowly stood up and said, "Mister, it is none of your business where I go. If this lady is willing to sit and talk with me, you better not interrupt us again."

Jud bellowed like a bull and charged up the steps.

Grady's right fist shot out like a striking snake striking Jud in the face. He flew backwards and put a dent in the dirt with his rear end. He coughed and got his breath back and then reached for his gun. It was then he realized he was looking right down the barrel of Grady's forty-four. "Mister if you want to live to see another sunrise you better take that hand away from that gun. I am not going to tell you twice."

Jud slowly got up from the ground. Boy, this is not the end of this, I'll see you again."

Grady waited until Jud was standing then lowered his gun back into the holster. "We can settle this right here, right now, if you are fool enough to try it."

Jud stared at him a minute but thought, *he is too confident.* He turned on his heels and almost ran back toward town.

Colleen walked into Mr. Thacker's office. "May I have a word with you?'

Laying a pencil in the fold of a large law book he said, "Certainly what can I do for you?"

"You know the mayor and the city board don't you?"

"Yes I know them. Why do you ask?"

"This city has a problem and I have a solution, but I need your help. They don't know me, so I need you to help me."

"What type of problem are we talking about?"

"She reached in her satchel and pulled out some papers and spread them on his desk.

⊨⊨ ⊨⊨

The setting sun was painting the sky with beautiful shades of yellow and orange when Grady knocked on the door at the boarding house. When he knocked, Marleen opened the door.

"Marleen, would you care to go for a walk with me? The moon is going to be bright so it will be safe to walk a ways. He handed her another bouquet of flowers.

Sniffing the flowers she said, "Let me put these in a jar of water and, yes I would love to walk with you."

In a moment she was back with a shawl over her shoulders. "Mr. McCain where would you like to walk?"

"Since technically I'm your partner in the freight business you can call me Grady."

"Sir I am not your partner, Colleen is your partner."

"Well madam that might be technically correct, but if I remember correctly Colleen said, Marleen and I would like to invest in your freight business."

"Oh she did—did she? Thank you again for the flowers that was very thoughtful of you. You look very handsome. You make me feel rather shabby walking with you."

"Marleen, no one will ever say you look shabby. You would look beautiful dressed in a feed bag."

"Grady I don't believe that would be true but it was a nice thing for you to say" She slipped her hand in his elbow on his left side. As they walked she asked about the business. Then she asked about what it was like growing up in boy's town. He asked about the school she had been going to. They watched a beautiful sunset and then it was a beautiful night softly lighted by a full moon. Too soon they were back at the boarding house, he took both of her soft little hands in his big calloused hands and said "Since your father is not here for me to ask, I asked your sister for permission to court you properly. Now I ask you, do I have your permission to do this again?"

"How soon, would you like to do this again?"

"Tomorrow."

"Grady I would love that but don't you need your rest. After all you are working very hard all day?"

"My lady nothing restores my energy like walking with you. Tomorrow night I will bring a buggy and we can go for a ride in the moon light."

"Good night Grady. I will look forward to tomorrow night."

<hr />

Jud showed up the next morning at Mrs. Bradenton's house, knocked on the door. Mrs. Bradenton walked to the door, Jud whipped off his hat, "Good morning Mrs. Bradenton. I would like to talk with Marleen."

"Just a moment."

A few minutes Marleen came to the door.

"Good morning my beauty. Can I come in and talk a minute?"

"No you cannot. Why didn't you tell me that the rail road was paying my sister for the lease to lay tracks across the Hill Valley ranch?"

Jud was momentarily stunned by the sudden change in Marleen. He figured after last night she would be feeling sorry for him by now. He recovered quickly, "Darling that is just business, I see no reason to worry your pretty head with such trivial matters. After we're married I'll take care of all such matters and you'll never have to think about business matters ever again."

"Jud you are a liar and a fraud. I will never marry you, not now not ever. Good day." She closed the door.

Furious he stormed off the porch. "It's that stupid Grady, everything was going great until he showed up. I'm gonna kill that waif if I don't do anything else. No matter how all this turns out I'm gonna kill Grady McCain."

Two weeks later they were sitting on the swing in front of the boarding house when Marleen said, "Grady, I have decided I am not going back to school."

"No honey, you only lack one more year and you will graduate. Your father paid for this year and Colleen has the money for next year. That is why he borrowed the money from the bank. I will miss you every single day until school is out but you must go back and honor your father. Maybe at Christmas you can come back home or maybe Colleen and I can come to Boston to see you."

"Grady I don't want to go back to school I want to stay here. I can't go a whole year without seeing you every day. It would be impossible."

He took her in his arms and gently pulled her to him, he loved the smell of her hair, she had washed it with rose water. "Darling I will write to you every day. I want you to write me a letter every day and tell all about what life is like in Boston and then before you know it school will be out and you'll be home. We'll have the grandest wedding Texas has ever seen."

"Oh Grady, I'll do it if you want me to, but I don't want to go. Do you promise you will write to me every day?"

"Yes my love, I promise. "

"Grady McCain, if I go two days without a letter from you, I will be on the next train leaving Boston. Do you hear me?"

Laughing he said, "Okay my fiery little redhead I hear you and I believe you. I will write a letter everyday but give me three days before you jump on a train in case the post office is delayed."

CHAPTER THIRTY-NINE

Two weeks later Colleen walked in and said, "Grady I need to talk to you a minute."

"So what brings you out here? Are we out of money?"

"Oh, lord no. We have plenty of money in the bank."

"What then?"

"Grady, remember when I had another idea."

"I knew it. I told Marlene I was waiting for the next horse shoe to fall. What have you got us into now? Although I will say partner, everything you have gotten us into has paid off very well."

"Remember when I said every time it rains that street through town gets to be a mud bog quickly."

She then outlined the program for him again.

"The city council has approved it."

"Let me make sure I understand what you're saying. The sheriff would basically put the prisoners on a chain gang to load rock for us to haul back to town and he would put another chain gang in town to unload and spread it. We would furnish the wagons and drivers. They would pay us $50.00 per load and you think each wagon can make four loads a day. What am I missing? How many loads would it take?

"Well I suggested that we haul enough to cover all of Main Street for about three hundred feet. Just the center part of town. The town council and the county now wants us to cover a whole mile a half mile on either side of town."

"How many loads are we talking about?"

"Each load only covers about ten feet from side to side."

"Have you calculated how many loads that will be?"

"Yes, between five hundred and six hundred."

"Who owns that cliff where you plan to harvest the rock?"

"We do, now."

"Colleen, how much did that cost us?"

"$500.00. The guy thought I was a dumb little redheaded girl, it was worthless land, all rock, and you couldn't grow anything on it so he sold to me for $500.00. I figure we'll make $1,200.00 the first day."

"Colleen, you're amazing. I thank God every day for meeting you O'Shanity girls. I often wish I could have known your dad. I saw him but never met him."

"You could have added and the prettiest partner in the world too." She said with a grin.

"Let's wait and see how this special delivery turns out and see if I think my partner is pretty." Grady laughed and said, "Let's ride out and have a look at this cliff of rock my partner has bought and see how pretty she looks after I get a look at where our money is going."

Jud was watching them as they climbed into the black carriage and started out of town.

Now I wonder where those two are going. I'll bet that ain't no social ride.

Soon Grady drove the carriage up to a sheer cliff of rock about forty feet high. "Colleen how are we supposed to chip that rock off that cliff and haul it into town?"

"I've been thinking about that, we can get some blasting powder and drill some holes in the cliff at the base and set off the blasting powder and the whole face should crumble and fall down. Then we could shovel it into the wagons and haul it to town. Men on that end could unload it and spread it while the wagons are going back for another load."

"How long will this job take?"

"If we use six wagons I figure while one is unloading another is being loaded. By using six wagons, we would have one wagon loading and one unloading all the time. We would have two coming and two going, so there would be a continuous stream of wagons being unloaded all day long. I think we can load a wagon in about thirty minutes and unload one in about the same time. We can haul twenty four loads in a twelve hour day so it will take us about five weeks to move six hundred wagon loads of rock."

"Okay if and that is a big if, we set the blast then the next day start hauling. You're not going to get six hundred loads out of one blast. When will we set the next blast? Do you plan on us working one day, blasting the next day, so we will be hauling rock every other day?"

"No Grady, we own the cliff face for a half mile in each direction. I would set the first charges close to the west end and while they are hauling from that end I would be drilling blasting holes here in the center. I would slowly work my way down the face of the cliff going from west to east. "

"When did you become a mining engineer?'

"I'm not but Mr. Thacker introduced me to Mr. Bixby who is an engineer and I've been talking to him." She took off her bonnet and fanned her face. "Let's get started back to town, it's hot just sitting here with no breeze."

"Colleen, we are making plenty of money now. What're you going to do with all this money?"

"I've been thinking."

"Oh that doesn't surprise me."

"I've been thinking when Marleen gets back she and I could start a finishing school here in west Texas so young ladies won't have to go all the way to Boston for college."

"What about boys?'

"They have an Agricultural and Mechanical college for young men down in the little town of Bryan Texas. This would be for young women. If it's alright with you."

"Have you talked to Marleen about this?"

"No."

"What if she doesn't want to do it, after all she will be getting married when she finishes school, you know."

"If she doesn't want to do it we won't do it. I'll think of something else."

"I have another question. If I am going to spend a month hauling rock for the road, who will be seeing that the freight is getting delivered?"

"Well I've been thinking about that. If you put Ronnie out there to supervise the mining and hauling of the rock and put Lonnie in charge of seeing that the freight gets delivered, then you can bounce back and forth between each job and it should go well."

"Colleen we'll be spread awfully thin. What if one of them gets hurt or gets sick? Then where would we be?"

⫘⫘

CHAPTER FORTY

The two men from the railroad stepped in removing their hats, "Good morning Miss O'Shanity, Mr. Thacker."

"Good morning gentlemen. Miss O'Shanity has no idea what this meeting is about. I thought it best if you presented your idea yourself."

"Very well. Miss O'Shanity first let me ask you, how is your freight business doing?"

"Very well thanks to you. We have three new wagons coming in soon and Grady is in the process of hiring three new mule skinners."

"Miss O'Shanity as you know the government has deeded land to the railroad along the right of way to be used as we see fit to facilitate the railroad. We would like to lease to you and Grady one hundred acres, south of the railroad depot to build a first class warehouse and livery barns for your mule teams. We would also like for you to construct holding pens for cattle being held for loading on the next available train."

"How much rent will we have to pay for this land?"

"How about we give you a fifty year lease for the sum of $1.00 a year?"

"Did you say $1.00?"

"Yes. Then you are supposed to build stock holding pens and loading chutes."

"How soon do you want those pens built? Who pays for the lumber and men to build the chutes?"

"You would of course."

"So you are a fraud sir. You said my rent on the land would be $50.00 for fifty years. When in fact it would be many times over that when I factor in the cost of building and maintaining those chutes."

"Miss O'Shanity, I object a little bit to the term fraud. I do see how it might look that way, however there is something I haven't told you. You will be allowed to charge $1.00 per head for all cattle shipped from those pens."

"Thank you, I apologize if I'm a little abrupt at times in business. When do you expect the first shipment of cattle to arrive?"

"The 888's ranch will have a shipment ready in thirty days."

"How many head of cattle are they planning to ship?"

"About four-thousand head."

"That's a lot of beef. It's going to be almost impossible to take care of the business and get that many cattle pens built in thirty days. I've got a lot of confidence in Grady. If anybody can do it's him. We would love to do it for you. I want the railroad to pay me the $4,000.00 now before the cattle get here so we will have the funds to purchase the material and hire the manpower to complete the project on time."

"Be reasonable young lady. The railroad is giving you a tremendous deal already. You cannot expect them to pay for the building and then pay you $1.00 for every head of cattle shipped from our own pens."

"Then you will have to get someone else. Let me remind you that our contract says we have the exclusive right to handle all freight shipments within a fifty mile radius of Abilene."

"That doesn't include cattle."

Colleen looked at Mr. Thacker and said, "Do you see anything in there that says live stock is excluded?"

"No as a matter of fact I do not. It simply says all freight. Which I suspect the court would rule includes cattle shipped."

"There you are gentlemen. If you don't want to do the deal my way then you need to go fifty-one miles down the track and build your cattle pens there."

The two railroad men whispered to each other and then one said, "Miss O'Shanity, I'm going to stop referring to you as a lady. That is an insult to a tough business woman like yourself. You are a lady, at all other time but not when you are negotiating. I'll have you a bank draft for $4,000.00 tomorrow. It will be a draw against future shipments."

Colleen smiled and said, "Well if it will make you feel any better. We will let the railroad bring us all the lumber and material we need to build the pens and barns."

All three men laughed.

Mr. Thacker said, "Are you going to have your attorney draw up the lease?"

"Yes we'll get it sent out on tomorrow's mail run."

"Good, I want to read it before either one of them sign it."

One of the railroad men said, "Well now that we have that finished there is something else we want to ask. Now I'm afraid to find out what this is going to cost us."

CHAPTER FORTY-ONE

J ud said. "I am not going to answer any more questions until my lawyer gets here."

The sheriff told one of the deputies, "Put him in a cell and send word to his lawyer. He'll give you the man's name." He then turned to the marshal, "We may as well go get some lunch. The lawyer will want to talk to his client for a few minutes. Then we'll see what kind of plea deal he wants to make."

"As far as I'm concerned I don't care if the judge hangs the arrogant louse."

"I guess you heard about a couple of outlaws tried to steal one of Grady's wagons loaded with furs the other day?" The sheriff said.

"No what happened?"

"According to Ronnie he picked up a load of furs from the tanner and was bringing them back to the depot when two guys with bandanas over their faces stopped 'em. They told Grady and Ronnie to get down they were taking the wagon and load. The man on the right had his gun out, the one on the left had not drawn his gun. Grady whispered to Ronnie you take the one on the left and he turned like he was getting ready to climb down.

Then a forty-four appeared in his hand and shot the dude right out of the saddle."

"Grady drew on a man with a drawn gun?"

"That takes some guts. Ronnie said he never saw him reach for a gun it just appeared in his hand and it was shootin'."

"Jacob trained him. In fact Jacob gave him that gun. He always said Grady had the best hand and eye coordination he had ever seen and the boy was fast as lightening."

"Well we might as well mosey back over there and see what the shyster lawyer has to offer."

When the two officers walked in a small bald man with weasel eyes handed each of them a card, and said, "I am Hershel Abernathy and I demand that you release my client immediately."

⊱ ⊰

Marleen came to the door and said, "My goodness Grady. You look very nice. Are those for me?"

"They are," he handed the flowers to her.

She smelled the honeysuckle and said, "You don't need to bring me flowers every time you come. Thank you, I love the way the honeysuckle smells. Come in and have a seat while I find a jar to put these in. I love the way you arranged the red and yellow Indian Paint Brushes in a circle with a fountain of white honeysuckle coming out of the top, very pretty. Did you get my sister to arrange these for you?"

"No Colleen doesn't know I brought those to you."

She was back in a few minutes and said, "Let's sit out on the porch and talk it's nice outside this evening."

When they were seated side by side on the wooden porch bench Marlene asked, "How is the partnership doing? Colleen never talks to me about it."

Grady told her all about the new wagons they had on order, he did not mention the attempted hold up.

"Isn't it dangerous traveling up and down all those roads, one man by himself?"

"Maybe a little bit but each driver has a six-shooter and a rifle or shot gun with him. When possible we send two or more wagons together. For instance if we have three deliveries to Albany we send all three at the same time so they can look out for each other."

They talked about the summer being almost over and it was time for her to go back to school.

She said, "Grady I don't think I'm going to go back. So much has happened. I don't think I want to go back to school."

"Marlene, if you do go back I am going to miss you a lot. I've known this since the first time I ever called on you. I wish I could spend every minute with you between now and then but I can't. I have to be on a wagon seat at first light and I don't get back until after dark a lot of days. I hardly see Colleen and she's my partner. Let me tell you she is an awesome partner. That woman is a business woman."

"So you really like her?"

"Yes as a partner and a friend, but I am not attracted to her like I am to you. Not in the same way. No."

"Why is that?'

He thought for a moment before saying, "Colleen is very pretty, you are beautiful, Colleen is tough and smart, you are kind and caring. Remember when you took care of that little bird? You are intelligent she is smart. The two of you are both amazing."

CHAPTER FORTY-TWO

"Why should we release the prisoner right now?"

"Because you have no grounds on which to hold him. No judge is going to let you go to trial. You have nothing."

"Oh is that right?" The marshal said, "I have a man who was murdered in his bed. A paralyzed man I might add."

Holding up his index finger he said "Your client has a motive."

Holding up his second finger he said, "We can place him at the scene of the murder. We have a link off his gold watch chain that is missing the big gold nugget that always hung on the end of it."

Holding up the next finger he said, "Your client jumped up at first light the morning after the murder was committed before anyone else even knew the man was dead and rushed off a wire to an attorney in Austin instructing him to immediately file the papers to take possession of the deceased man's property. Why was he in such a hurry? Was it because he wanted it done before anyone found out the man was dead?"

The lawyer scoffed, "its guys like you that make my job easy."

Holding his index finger he said, "Just because you have some saloon gal saying she overheard a conversation between who knows who. They sure couldn't see through the wall."

Holding up the next finger. "Jud lost the gold nugget in a poker game three months ago. He lost it to a drummer (traveling salesman) passing through town."

Holding up the third finger he said, "Maybe the drummer is your man."

Then he closed the first and third finger down leaving just the middle finger sticking up and said, "That's your case. Turn the man lose."

The two officers looked at each other and the sheriff told one of the deputies, "Release the prisoner."

Jud came walking out. He looked like he started to say something. The marshal said, "I'm still convinced you are guilty and I will come and find you again when I have more proof. Your fast talking lawyer is not going to get you out of this. We are not through."

The lawyer grabbed Jud and said, "Don't say a word. Let's get out of here."

As soon as they were outside Jud said, "I hate those two. I feel like going back in there and gunning them both down."

"That'll get you hung quicker than anything I can think of. Come on over to the saloon let me buy you a drink, you need to calm down."

"I don't want a drink. I want a woman and I know the one I want."

He stormed off down the street.

Grady and Marlene were sitting on the porch talking when Jud came storming up. "Get away from my fiancé."

Grady looked at Marlene "Jud, you know I am not your fiancé."

"Why you little two faced hussy."

As soon as the words were out of his mouth, Grady was on his feet and in two long strides his work hardened right fist smashed into Jud's face. Jud's hat flew ten feet across the yard. He landed flat on his back in the dirt. He lay there for a stunned second then come off the ground bellowing like an angry bull.

Colleen went back into the lawyer's office and he had the papers on his desk for her to sign. "I have read the documents. There is nothing in there that I object too. You can go ahead and sign it, if that is still what you want."

The railroad men came in together, "Good morning Miss O'Shanity, and you councilor."

"Colleen said you mentioned you had something else you wanted to talk about. May I suggest we dispense with this matter," pointing to the documents on the desk, "Before we talk about anything else. You are very direct and get right to the point. In a strange sort of way I like that. I like doing business with you because we don't have to beat around the bush. I believe we can trust anything you tell us to be true."

"Certainly. I am not in the habit of telling lies. If I don't like something I tell you. So far you have also been men of your word. Grady and I are partners who are both cut from the same cloth. If he tells you something you can take it to the bank."

"We have found that to be true so far." The documents were passed around and signed, when they were passed back to the attorney he kept a copy for Grady and Colleen and handed the other to the railroad men. They passed a check to him.

"Miss O'Shanity we have a shipment coming soon that is going to be extremely valuable and extremely sensitive. It will endanger many lives if this is leaked out. So absolute secrecy is paramount. I must tell you before we came to talk with you we had Pinkerton check out both you and Grady. Their report is very favorable."

"Sir, what are you talking about? We are in the business of hauling freight. Why all the secrecy?"

"Miss O'Shanity, we are talking about hauling over $100,000.00 cash money. The government is experimenting with setting up a federal reserve bank. A central bank that all other banks can borrow money from and loan out to farmers, ranchers, businesses. They have chosen this area as a test to see if it will stimulate the economy. If the test is successful then in a few years it will be all over the nation. All banks will not be limited to only the money their depositors have in the bank."

"I am confused. You are going to ship money on the train? You want us to haul to the banks? Is it going to be gold?"

"No it will be dollar bills so the weight should not be a problem."

"How much money are we talking about?"

"$200,000.00"

Colleen gasped and said, "Did you say $200,000.00."

"I didn't know they had that much money to ship anywhere."

"This is being done very secretly, because for that much money there are governments that would be tempted to send armed troops to take it from you. There are gangsters in New York that would send henchmen by the droves. There are plenty of local bank robbers that have never seen a load of cash like this. What do you say?"

"I don't know. What does it pay? Surely we can't take that kind of risk for normal freight rates."

One of the railroad men turned to the other and said, "Didn't I tell you? This lady doesn't miss a thing."

"No. The United States government is going to advance you $2,000.00 to build a special wagon to haul this money. Every driver you hire will have to be checked out by both Pinkerton and the US Army before he can be hired."

Colleen immediate thought of Jud, wouldn't he love to get his hands on this shipment. "When is this shipment supposed to come?"

"In two months."

"So you are saying the first of October then?"

"That is correct."

"Now back to my original question. How much to haul this load of cash?"

"You will be paid $2,000.00 now to build the wagon to the specifications the government has required. Then you will be paid an agreed to amount for each shipment."

CHAPTER FORTY-THREE

Jud rushed Grady and tried to grab him in a bear hug. Grady danced back and slammed a hard left into Jud's belly, followed immediately by another right fist to his face. Jud's face was now a bloody mess, from his smashed nose and lips. Jud backed off and grabbed for his gun. Before he could even get it out of the holster he realized he was looking down the barrel of a forty-four. His hand froze and the gun dropped back in the leather.

Jud bellowed, "I'll get both of you for this."

The next sound he heard was the metallic click of a gun being cocked. "Jud if you ever even speak to this lady again I will kill you like the dog you are."

Jud turned and ran down the street. Whimpering as he ran.

Grady calmly lowered the gun back into his holster and walked back to the swing where Marlene still sat.

She said, "Grady I don't know what to say. I never saw that side of him before. He was always so kind and a gentleman. He took me on a nice picnic the other day and was a perfect gentleman. I thought he spoke pretty words. Not as pretty as you though. You are the first boy or man to bring me flowers in my life. Do you think he will try again to get you like he said?"

"It's not me I'm worried about. I heard him say 'I will get both of you.' If he comes after me I'll handle him. The man is a bully but deep down he is a coward. Did you see how he ran? What if he really is the one who killed your father? Putting a pillow over a paralyzed man's face is a cowardly thing to do."

She started to cry softly.

Grady put his arm around her shoulders, "Don't cry darling. Everything is going to be alright. We are making more money than Colleen or I even dreamed we could. I would like to come back and take some walks together, in the moon light, if that's okay with you."

"Oh Grady I feel like such a fool. I considered marrying Jud because it looked like the only way to support Colleen. Then you solved that problem. Jud was pressuring me to get married. I kept stalling. I'm glad you weren't hurt. I kept thinking how I felt when I watched you and Lonnie fight. It was horrible. I kept wanting them to stop the fight I didn't care who won."

"Hey girl, there at the end I was thinking the same thing."

They both smiled. Grady leaned over and kissed her gently on the lips.

"Is this a onetime deal? Will there be just one shipment of cash to be distributed to several banks in this region?" Colleen asked.

Mr. Thacker said, "That's a good question Colleen."

The railroad man said, "No, there will be shipments once a moth. Depending on which banks have loaned out the first batch of money. This first shipment will be the largest. Because money will be going to all of the chosen banks. After that it will be delivering money to those who have used up their first allotment."

Colleen sat thinking for a moment then said, "You still haven't answered my original question. If we are going to risk the lives of our drivers and our equipment, we will not do that for regular freight rates. So back to my question. How much for the first haul and how much for each additional haul?"

"I'm authorized to offer you from $500.00 up to $1,000.00 for the first trip. Since I know how you negotiate, I will simply jump to the $1,000.00 number now."

"No. My men's lives are worth more than that, I want $2,000.00."

"That is out of the question ma'am we can get the army to do it if you refuse."

Colleen turned and looked at the lawyer and said. "Is there anything in our contract that allows the army to deliver freight within our area?"

"No."

"If you are going to make us adhere to every word in that contact, then I am going to suggest that the railroad start looking at everything you are doing. You may be in violation of something. If you refuse to cooperate we may be forced to sue."

Colleen looked at the lawyer and said, "When will the judge be back in town?"

He looked at his calendar and said, "Next week."

"Good, contact the secretary of the court and put this matter on his calendar and demand a jury trial."

"Now wait a minute Miss O'Shanity, I didn't say we were going to sue. I said we might sue."

Colleen looked at the two railroad men and said, "The first load goes to twenty different banks. Is that right?"

"Yes."

"Then here is my proposal. We will get paid $2000.00 for the first load which is probably the least dangerous even though it is the most money. If we keep it secret the bad guys won't know it's here. It will not take them long to figure out that there is a load of money coming off that train every month. So I want $200.00 for each bank we deliver to after the first load."

"Miss O'Shanity. I will not pay you $200.00 for the two banks here in Abilene."

"Let me talk to Grady and I'll let you know tomorrow morning. Can we meet here again tomorrow?"

"You are the most exasperating person I have ever dealt with. Fine, you talk to your partner and we'll meet here tomorrow, what time?"

Colleen turned to the lawyer and said, "What time is convenient for you?"

He looked at his calendar and said, "I have another client coming in at 8:30. I should be available by 9:30."

The railroad men said, "Let's make it 10:00 to be sure."

Colleen looked at the attorney who nodded his head, she said, "Okay gentlemen. I will have you an answer tomorrow. So we are all on the same page. We are not talking about if we'll haul the money. We're talking about how much is that service worth to you and the government."

After a few pleasantries they all agreed to meet tomorrow at 10:00 o'clock.

As Colleen walked out of the office the younger of the two railroad men said "Not only is that woman one of the most beautiful women I have ever known, she is also one of the smartest."

The older man said, "She is sharp. Thank God, everybody we meet is not like her, it would make our job a whole lot harder."

"What're you going to do if she comes back and insists on $200.00 for every drop off?"

CHAPTER FORTY-FOUR

J ud was stomping around the front room of the ranch house
with a bottle of whiskey in his hand. Who would've thought we
could lose a herd of 2000 cattle. Why would a bunch of sheriff's
deputies be out riding at night? How could that stupid kid from
the orphanage talk Marlene into refusing to marry me? I had her
in the palm of my hand after the picnic. That smart mouth older
one and that dude have bought some wagons and now they are in
the freight business. He took a big swallow and continued pacing.
They even have a contract with the railroad.

I heard somebody in the saloon say they are making a lot of
money already.

I hear the railroad is gonna build a lot of loading pens out
there, I'll round up another bunch of beef and ship them on the
train. That way if something happens to them the railroad will
have-ta pay me. So I get my money either way.

He reached up and rubbed his jaw which was still sore. I'm
gonna kill that kid. He sucker punched me so he could make himself look good in front of that gal. I can shoot a hole in a dime from

100 yards with my Winchester. I'll get him. He won't be the first man I have had to eliminate. Now that I think about it, all my bad luck started after that kid showed up.

⊷⊱ ⊰⊶

Grady showed up at the boarding house, "Good evening Mrs. Bradenton's, is Colleen in?"

"Yes she is. I tell you that girl works all the time. She has those books out going over'em every time I knock on her door. Have a seat while I go tell her you're here."

"Tell her I'll have a seat out here in the old rocking chair, it's nice out this evening."

Colleen came out and said, "How did today go?"

"It went well. One of the teamsters had a minor brush with three or four Comanche over near the gap. A few sprinkles of buck shot from his scatter gun discouraged them. One of the mules is going lame a little. I'm going to pull him and put one of the spares in for a few days. I hired a man to grease all of the axel hubs every night. What have you got that we need to talk about?"

"Thank you for standing up for Marlene."

"That fool came charging up here and ordered me to leave. Called her his fiancé. She told him she was not his fiancé. I was mad because he interrupted us. We were having a fine conversation. Then he called her a hussy. So I wholoped him. He tried to pull a gun, but changed his mind when he realized he was looking down the barrel of my forty-four."

"Marlene said y'all had a fight."

"It wasn't no fight. He never hit me, I just knocked him down, and then he tried to pull a gun and realized I already had mine in my hand before he got his out of the holster. Then he turned tail and ran."

"Grady I met with the railroad people again this morning over at Mr. Thacker's office. We have the contract to build loading pens out by the depot to ship cattle. We will get paid $1.00 for every steer shipped from our pens."

"How much're we going to have-ta pay for the land?"

"That's the good part. The government gave the railroad all the un-deeded land for a half mile on either side of the tracks. So they are going to lease one hundred acres to us. So we can build the holding pens. Which will take about ten acres. We can use the rest of it any way we want."

"That sounds great. You still haven't told me how much it's gonna cost."

"Grady, I'm glad you're sitting down because it's gonna cost us $1.00 a year for fifty years. So I say we go ahead and pay all fifty years in advance."

"Good Lord woman, are you saying we can get one hundred acres near the depot for $50.00?"

"Yes."

"How much do you figure it's gonna cost to build those holding pens?"

"About $2,000.00."

"Have we got that much? I don't worry about how much we have because I know you're taking care of that side of the business."

"We do, but it doesn't matter. The 888 Ranch is going to be our first customer and they are bringing four thousand head. So I talked the railroad into paying us the $4,000.00 in advance so we could build the holding pens."

"The railroad is going to give us the land for $50.00 and they are going to give us $4,000.00. Colleen you're amazing."

"If I have to build that many holding pens I'm going to have-ta get busy. When're we expecting the herd to get here?"

She grinned and said, "One month."

"What, did you say one month? Now you have gone crazy. We haven't even cleared the land or ordered the lumber or post."

"Well we sort-a have. I told them my partner was an amazing man and he could accomplish things that most people would think impossible."

"Colleen O'Shanity, don't you try your Irish blarney on me. When I said we haven't even ordered the lumber or post you said, well we sorta have. What does that mean?"

"The railroad engineers already have the plans drawn up. They are bringing all the material we will need on the morning train."

Grady's mouth dropped open.

She said, "Don't be mad. You were gone to the springs and I had to make a split second decision. Since they were paying us $4,000.00. I figured it was not much risk to pay $1,200.00 for the material. That still leaves $800.00 for labor and $2,000.00 profit."

"I don't know how I got so lucky to get you for a partner. What happens if I don't get the pens built in time?"

"Well they did mention something about a tall tree and a short rope."

"You, Miss Smarty Pants may have to be out there driving nails, or driving a freight wagon while I'm out there building pens. I think I better go get me some supper and get to sleep. I may not get much of either in the next month."

"Now Grady you'll have to admit this business of running a business is kind-a fun."

"I think it's a lot of fun for you and a lot of work for me. Don't make any more deals until we get this straightened out."

"Well there is one other thing."

CHAPTER FORTY-FIVE

The marshal and the sheriff sat down at a table over in the corner at May's. "It's a funny thing. Our friend Jud, seems to have some problems. I hear that he started a herd on the way to Fort Worth, and lightning struck the herd. Killed several steers and scattered the whole herd over half the state of Texas. Remember I've got three of his guys in jail for rustling. They told one of my deputies that three of his guys got caught in the stampede. Two men tried to high jack one of Grady's wagons loaded with furs from the tanner. Grady shot one of 'em out of the saddle and then told the other one to pick up the trash off the road and if he ever saw him within fifty yards of one of his wagons again he was gonna shoot him on sight. So Jud's getting short of gun slingers. "

"Well as long as he's shorthanded he can't cause as much mischief."

The sheriff laughed and said, "You've got a good point there. How are things here in town?"

"It's been pretty quiet just the normal Saturday night puncher who had one drink too many and wanted to fight everybody in town. We have-ta throw him in jail until he sleeps it off before somebody hurts'im."

They both laughed. Then the marshal said, "There was one thing. Ole Jud went over to see the younger O'Shanity gal right after we turned him lose and that young fellow Grady was over there talking to her. He tried to run the kid off and got his tail whipped."

"I saw that boy fight in the ring that time, he's a scrapper."

"Yeah and I heard that Jud tried to draw a gun on him and before he could get it out of the leather, he found himself looking right down the business end of a forty-four."

"The kid didn't shoot 'im?"

"No from what I hear Jud yelled some threats to them and then turned tail and ran."

"Jud's luck is gonna run out one of these days. If the kid had shot him as long as there was a witness who saw Jud reach first. Grady would have been justified."

"What kind-a threats did he make?"

Colleen said, "They have a special shipment coming in that is going to pay us $2.000.00 to deliver and about $1000.00 every month."

"Where do we have-ta haul it to Montana?"

"No, just around here in our area."

"Who are we hauling it to?"

"Several banks in the different towns around our area."

"Colleen you're killing me. What're we going to be hauling, gold?"

"No, we'll be hauling $200,000.00 in cash."

"Are you crazy there's not that much money in the world?"

She took time to explain the whole program to him.

"I guess you've already agreed to this too."

"No, in light of the fact that we are already committed to building the cattle loading pens, I told them I had to talk to you and that I would give them an answer tomorrow."

"Well that was nice of you."

"You'll have to admit it is a lot of money."

"How much money do we have in the bank right now?"

"About $5,000.00."

CHAPTER FORTY-SIX

Jud woke up hung over. Stumbled to the messy kitchen. *We need a woman around here to clean this mess up.* He opened the door on the wood stove and threw in a couple of sticks of fire wood. Bent down and blew on the coals from last night's fire until he had a blaze going. Then he put water on to boil for coffee. *I'm gonna kill that Grady dude. Then I'm gonna grab one of them O'Shanity gals and drag her out here chain her up so she can't get away until I'm tired of her. In fact I might get'em both. They think they're too good.*

One of the three men he had left walked in, and said, "Jud, we've gotta come up with some way to get some money. We're out of everything. Whiskey, tobacco, you name it."

"Well if you two hadn't botched that wagon job we could have sold them furs for a lot of money."

"Yeah, well I ain't never seen a man shuck a six-gun as fast as he did. One second Chuck had his gun trained on that dude and the next Chuck was blasted out of his saddle. Man I'll telling you that dude was like a magician. One second his gun is in its holster and the next second it was spitting fire and lead."

Jud shivered when he remembered looking right down the barrel of a forty-four that suddenly appeared in Grady's hand. What did that dude look like?"

"He was young. He couldn't ah been over twenty or twenty-one. He was a little taller than me, but not much, had reddish brown hair, and he had a gun that if had been any bigger it would've had wheels under it."

"That must have been Grady. Was there two men on the wagon?"

"Yes there was a really big guy driving."

"That dude with the gun was Grady. He and that oldest O'Shanity gal own all those wagons you see running around here."

"The same one we saw fight in that ring?"

"Yep."

"Well Jud, I've seem him fight and I've seen him shoot and I don't want no part of that hombre. In fact he told me if he sees me within fifty yards of one of his wagons he's gonna start shootin'. I ain't going anywhere near one of them wagons. I believe him. I'll rob a stage coach or a bank but I ain't messing with one of them red wagons with yeller wheels."

"He'll get what he's got coming to him one of these days," Jud said.

⋖⊹⊹⋗

"You and Marlene are still living in a boarding house and I'm still sleeping in a hay loft. I'll agree to this insane undertaking, if."

"If what?"

"That big white house around the corner on Hickory Street is for sale. You can buy it for $1,600.00. As crazy as this is I'll take on both projects if you'll draw out $1,600.00 and buy that house. I want you and Marlene to have a home."

"Oh my-gosh Grady. I've been looking at that house, dreaming about owning it. Are you sure we are ready? Wait a minute. We can't move into a nice house like that and have you still sleeping in a barn."

180

"I already thought of that. I am going to build a warehouse on the land you leased from the railroad. In one corner of the warehouse I'm going to build a nice apartment for a bachelor to live. I'll only be sleeping in the hay loft for a few more days until I can get all of this construction done that my partner keeps getting me into."

"First of all, we--- leased the land. Have you already talked to Marlene about this?"

"No because I didn't know we were ready to do it until now. I have another question for you. How would you feel if I asked Marlene to marry me?"

She was quiet for a minute before she said, "I'd love to see you two married. There's no one I would like to see my sister marry more than you. There's no one I would like to see you marry more than her. You already seem like a brother to me. That would make it official. I would like to see her go back to school and finish her last year. Daddy borrowed that money to pay for this year in school. I have enough to pay for next year. It would be such a waste to lose the ranch and then not finish the last year. Would it be asking too much if you could wait until she finishes her last year at school?"

Grady said, "I haven't asked her yet. What if she says no?"

"She won't say no to marrying you but she might say no to school. I want you to promise me, you'll do your best to talk her into going. Will you do that?"

"If my future sister-in- law, partner keeps making deals, I may not have time to get married anyway. Yes I'll ask Marlene to marry me and I'll ask her to wait until she finishes her last year at school. You know it's going to kill me to put her on a train knowing I want see her for a year."

"Maybe we could go up and spend Christmas with her. It would be fun to see snow at Christmas."

"Alright, I'll come back tomorrow night with my courting duds on and see what she says. If she tells me no, tou're going to have a very sad partner. If she refuses to go back to school, you can't hold it against me. I 'll do my best to sell the idea to her."

CHAPTER FORTY-SEVEN

The next evening Grady showed up at the boarding house with his new corduroy pants, new white shirt and polished boots on. Driving a buggy Mr. Bledsoe loaned him. Marlene and Mrs. Bradenton were sitting on the porch enjoying the cool breeze.

"Why Marlene, I believe there's a handsome young gentleman coming to call on you. Unless of course he's coming to call on me."

Grady felt his face getting hot, "no Mrs. Bradenton, you are looking quite lovely tonight, but tonight I would like to take Marlene for a ride in my buggy."

"Marlene he's not only a handsome gentleman, he's full of Irish blarney. Go on Marleen you two have a good time."

As he helped Marlene into the buggy seat she said, "Grady where are we going?"

"You asked me how the business was going. I want to show you something."

He drove out to the site where two freight cars were parked on the siding. They contained a mountain of lumber and post. "Your amazing sister and my amazing partner has made a deal with the railroad to lease us one hundred acres of land. We'd have right to all the land starting right here and going west for one half of a mile. That lumber is for me to build loading pens for all of the cattle to be shipped on the train from here."

"WOW! Colleen did that?"

"We are going to get paid $1.00 for every cow shipped out of these pens when they are finished."

"How soon will you be able to start shipping?"

The triple eight ranch is bringing four- thousand head in one month."

"You have got to get all of that built in one month?"

"I'm also going to build a large warehouse building over there by those cedar trees. In it I'm going to build a nice apartment for a bachelor to live in."

"Does that mean you won't be sleeping in the hayloft anymore?"

"Yes."

"That is wonderful. I have been worried about you sleeping up there in that smelly old barn."

"Now I have something else to show you and I want to ask you to do something for me." He snapped the reins and started the team back toward town.

"You are being awfully mysterious. What else are you planning to show me?"

He smiled and said "Look at that beautiful sunset. Did you have sunsets like that back east where you went to school?"

Marlene said, "It is beautiful. No, back east there are a lot more hills and a lot more trees. So you don't get quite the same effect as you do out here."

Soon Grady turned down Hickory Street and pulled up in front of a gorgeous white house with a large wrap around front porch. "How do you like this house?"

"I love it. Why are you showing it to me?"

"Because Colleen and I bought it today."

"You did. Why?"

"Because I can't have my partner and my future wife living in a boarding house."

"What did you say? Your what?"

"I said my partner and my future wife. Marlene darling will you marry me and become that future wife?"

She threw her arms around his neck and kissed him and said, "Grady McCain I was not expecting that. Yes, I will right away."

"Whoa, wait just a moment. There is one other thing I want you to say yes too."

"What? I am not going to drive a freight wagon after we get married."

He laughed and said, "No, I want you to agree to go back to school and finish your last year then hurry home as fast as the trains can bring you and marry me as soon as you step off the train."

"Grady, you can't be serious. Too much has happened I am not a school girl anymore."

Grady pulled her close to him and said, "Darling you are definitely not a school girl. You are the most beautiful woman I have ever seen. You are the woman I want to spend the rest of my life with. Your father mortgaged the ranch to pay for this year of school. In honor of him I would like to see you go finish the last year, Colleen has already paid the tuition. Then I want you to hurry home and be my bride. It will be the longest year of my life."

Tears flowed down her pretty face, "Grady that is the sweetest thing I have ever heard in my life. I don't know if I can stand it. To honor the sacrifices made by my dad, I am gonna try." She reached over and kissed him again.

"Well I couldn't stand to go a whole year without seeing you, so Colleen and I will be on the train to Boston, one week before Christmas. I've always wanted to see a white Christmas."

"Oh, is that the only reason you're coming to Boston in December?"

"No, the real reason I'm bringing your sister so you'll have a chaperone."

Marlene arched her eyebrow and said, "Maybe you should leave her here."

They both laughed and Grady said, "I'd like to see how you could accomplish that."

CHAPTER FORTY-EIGHT

The sheriff walked in and handed a letter to the marshal. "I've been making some inquiries about our man Jud. Read this," handing him a letter.

It was a letter from the US Marshal in Denver.

As to your inquiry about Jud Rawlins. He matches the description of a Jake Randell who is wanted here in Colorado. Randell is a narcissist, and a crooked gambler. He is the prime suspect in a scheme that bilked investors out of thousands of dollars by selling them stock in a mine that didn't exist.

He is also wanted for questioning about the mysterious death of a woman he was living with here in Denver.

⊷ ⊶

Colleen and Marlene moved into the new house. It was by far the grandest house they had ever lived in.

Marlene, said, "Colleen how are you ever going to keep this place clean?"

Before she could answer, Grady answered for her. "I have already thought of that, as soon as she turned that front room into an office for the freight company. So I hired an older lady to come in and cook and clean for you ladies."

"You hired somebody to work in my house without asking me?"

"Well technically it's half my house because the partnership money paid for it, and my future wife's going to be living here for a few more weeks."

Marlene laughed and said, "Big sister, he's got you there."

"Oh, so this's how it's gonna be. I'll have to put up with you two trying to gang up on me."

They both looked at each other and said, "Yep."

The next day Grady walked into Mr. Moskowitz's store. "Good afternoon sir what can I do for a fine young gentleman today?"

"I asked a girl to marry last night and she said yes. I would like to buy a diamond ring to put on her finger so she won't forget while she is back east finishing her school."

"Sir I have them from $50.00 to $500.00 what is your budget for rings today?"

"How about we settle in the middle say around $200.00?"

"An excellent choice. Tasteful enough to say you are special. Not expensive enough to frighten her with your extravagance. Let me show you three choices. I assure you she'll love, any of these three."

Grady put the small box in his pocket when he left the store. When he walked back into the livery stable he said, Mr. Bledsoe, I guess you need to sell me a horse and some tack. I can't keep borrowing yours, because I'm building a warehouse out on some land Colleen leased from the railroad. I'm building an apartment out there."

"Well that's a good thing. I'm proud of how good you're doing."

"Well are you proud enough to give me a good deal on a good horse?"

"Grady lesson number one when it comes to horse tradin' I ain't proud of nobody. I will see that you get a sound one though. Stay away from that black horse, He has a tendency to colic, now that little paint's a good horse for riding around town on short trips. If you want a horse that has bottom and will work all day with ya, get that Appaloosa."

"Mr. Bledsoe how much do you want for that Appaloosa?"

"$110.00."

"I'm gonna send Colleen over here she's the negotiator, not me."

"I don't care if you send the pope. That horse is $110.00."

"Okay you ole skin flint. Throw in one of them old broken down saddles out of the tack room and you've got a deal."

"I'll do better than that, I'll throw in a saddle and bridle."

Colleen and Marlene sat down at the table in their new home for the first time. "Let's ask the lord's blessing on this new house."

"Colleen it's not a house now it's a home."

"You are right. By the time you and Grady get married the business should have enough money that we can build you a new home anywhere around here you want it."

"Oh Colleen a year is a long time. I don't know if I can stand not seeing him for a year."

"You won't have to wait a year. We'll come at Christmas time. Maybe at Easter you can sneak off and come back for a few days. With modern railroads getting better and faster all the time, by Easter you might be able to get on a train on Friday morning and get off here on Saturday afternoon."

"That doesn't seem possible does it?"

"They say you can mail a letter to Boston in two days."

"You make sure that partner of yours remembers to write me a letter every day."

"Okay, but before we eat in our new home. Let's ask the Lord to bless this house."

They bowed their heads and Colleen said;

Lord we thank you for this nice home you have provided for us. It was just a few weeks ago when we lost our daddy and the world looked bleak and dark. Then Lord I opened my Bible and read your own words written long ago in., Proverbs 3:5-6 "Trust in the Lord with all your heart and lean not on your own understanding; in all your ways acknowledge him, and he will make your paths straight."

"Lord we trusted you and you have brought us out of homelessness to this fine home. You have brought me a fine decent hard working partner. You have brought Marlene a fine decent man to marry. Thank you, Lord, only you could make both of those in the same man.

Lord we give this fine house to you. We ask your blessings on it and every person who walks through these doors. Thank you for entrusting the care of your house to us. May we enjoy the blessing and pledge to use it only for your good.

In Jesus name.

Amen

CHAPTER FORTY-NINE

Jud got his guys together. "Boys I hear that the railroad is building holding pens and loading chutes here. We don't have to drive a herd all the way to Fort Worth. We can gather up a herd and put them on a train and have the money in our pocket within two days."

"Are they ready to ship now?"

"No, I understand they'll be ready in two weeks. Think we should start with a small herd. We 'll sweep up a couple of hundred head. We can handle that many by ourselves, and collect $3,000.00 or $4,000.00 to test the system. Let me get some money back in the bank, then we can hire some more guys and pull in a real herd."

"I keep thinking about that wagon load of furs. I wonder what else they haul in those wagons."

"Jud why don't you ask them gals in the saloon if they ever hear any talk about what they're hauling in them wagons."

"Slim that's a good idea. Them gals hear everything. Guys get a little liquored up and they start talking. Wantin' to impress the gal with what they know."

"I'll bet every one of those drivers frequent the saloon from time to time."

"I need to go see one of them women anyway. Got an itch that needs scratching."

"Just make sure you're the one listening, not the one talking." Both of Jud's men laughed.

CHAPTER FIFTY

Grady hired every able bodied man in town. He put ten or twelve building pens and fifteen or twenty building a warehouse, with sleeping quarters in it.

On the morning of the fourth day a train pulled in with the parts of a new wagon to be assembled. It was really different from any wagon anybody had ever seen.

One of the new men said, "What in the world is that?"

"I don't know but the parts sure are heavy. It's something to do with a wagon look at them wheels. They're the biggest, widest wheels I ever seen."

As soon as the crates came off the train, Grady moved them into the unfinished warehouse out of sight of anybody outside.

"It looks like Grady is puttin' together a heavy duty wagon. I wonder what he's gonna be ah hauling that's that heavy."

Later that evening the two men that unloaded the crates full of wagon parts were sipping a beer in the saloon. One of them said, "You know I'm still real curious what Grady's gonna be hauling on that new heavy duty wagon."

Jud overheard them talking and eased the gal off his lap. He sidled up to the two men and said, "I won big at the poker game earlier and I hate to celebrate all by myself. Why don't you guys split this bottle with me? My name is Jud and I own the H-V ranch out north of town."

"Who was you playing with?"

"I don't know just a bunch of drummers passing through town but boy did I get lucky. Drew an inside straight and cleaned up."

"That was luck, every time I tried that I busted."

"Are you guys' cowhands?"

"We're whatever it takes to catch the coon. We've worked a lot of cattle. Right now we're carpenters."

"Who's building a new house?"

"Ain't no new house, there's a fellow building some holding pens and loading chutes. He come looking for help. About that time we was looking for some money. So when he said he'd pay $2.00 a day we jumped on. That's better than being a $30.00 a month cow nurse."

"You ever drive one of them wagons?"

"Naw, we only been working there four days. I understand them, mule skinners get paid good money to drive a freight wagon."

"Yeah, I heard they get paid $5.00 a day. That's as much in one week as a cowhand makes in a month. "The other man said, "I ain't never drove one of them wagons but for $30.00 a week I'm willing to start."

"You two seem like smart men, I own the Hill-Valley ranch. If I decide you are somebody I can trust, I'll tell you how to make a lot more money than driving a freight wagon."

"What would we have–ta do?"

"You know all the stuff being hauled in them wagons is stuff rich folks ordered in or planned to ship out. If you was to keep your eyes open for something really unusual coming in or going on over there, I'll make it worth your while. Then if you bring me good information, maybe I can share some more information with you."

"Well, we saw something today that was kind ah unusual."

Jud refilled their glass and said, "What kind-ah unusual thing are you talking about?"

"Well we helped unload a lot of heavy crates. It looked like it was parts for a strange wagon."

"What do you mean by strange?"

"Well one thing the wheels were big and wide. We couldn't see what was in all of the crates but they was the heaviest crates I ever seen."

"How do you know it was a wagon then?"

"The wheels were not in a crate. They was just banded together. They couldn't put no wagon tongue in a crate."

"What do you suppose they're planning to haul in that wagon?"

"I don't know but it must be real heavy."

"Guys I'll pay you $20.00 a piece if you find out what that wagon is gonna be hauling. That'll be a good test. If you come through on this I'll let you in on a money making deal I got together."

"Mister you ain't expecting us to rob no banks are ya?"

"No you find out what that wagon is for and I'll let you in on a deal that'll have you struttin' around smoking cigars all day long."

CHAPTER FIFTY-ONE

Colleen and Marlene spent the day making and hanging sheer drapes on the windows facing the front porch. They hung pictures, and placed crocheted doilies under lamps and folded an afghan over the back of the divan. Slowly they were changing a beautiful house into a lovely home.

"Colleen it's too hot to fire up that stove. Why don't I go down to the farmer's market and get some fresh stuff for a big salad?"

"Okay while you are doing that I'll set a glass jar full of water and tea out in the sun and we can have a glass of sun tea in a little while. Are you comfortable walking down to the market all by yourself?"

"Colleen it's broad open day light in Abilene, Texas, sure I'm okay.

———

Jud walked out of the saloon, stopped and lit a cigar as the marshal walked up. "Evening marshal."

"Jud, I see you have your watch chain back."

"The jeweler put this silver dollar on it for me."

"Tell me again when and where you lost that gold nugget off the chain. It must have been worth $20.00."

Jud bristled, and said, "It was worth, over $50.00 and I lost it in a poker game."

"Over $50.00 in one pot is a pretty healthy game. How come I never heard about a game that rich going on here in town?"

"I guess, even a marshal has to sleep some times."

"That's a fact, you take care now Jud. I'll be seeing ya," the marshal said and walked away.

Jud's two new associates were working the next morning when one said, "I wonder what they are going to be hauling in that new wagon?"

"I don't know but it's worth $40.00 for us to find out."

"When we stop to eat lunch maybe I can mosey over there and see what I can find out."

"They've got the building pretty well closed up but they're leaving the doors open. I just can't see in there from here."

"Do you know anybody that's working over there?"

"That ole long legged boy over there, I worked a trail drive with him one time. You know how it is on a trail drive we didn't have much time for socializing. His name is Ed, I'll kind-ah wander up there and talk about that drive and see if I can get any information about what it is they're building in there."

"You could hear the sound of hammers echoing all over the area. Men were building, the pens and the warehouse." Grady looked and thought, *it's all coming together. When Colleen first told me I was going to have-ta build these pens, I thought I can do that. Then she told me I needed to build the warehouse, I thought wow, I guess I can do that too. Then when she threw in that armored wagon. I thought, there ain't no way I can get all that done.*

He looked down at the dog standing in his shadow and said, "Just think Knot in a few days we'll have four-thousand head of bawling steers in those pens. You and I won't be sleeping in a hay barn anymore."

The work stopped for lunch. Jenkins ambled over to where the men building the warehouse were spreading their lunch in the shade of the building. "Hello Ed. I thought that was you. Remember me we did that trail drive for old Swartz that time?"

"Howdy Jenkins what ya been up to?"

"Oh, just trying to make enough money to keep body and soul together. I was hanging around looking for some work when this fellow showed up saying he was hiring some fellows to build stock pens. So here I am. What about you?"

"Pretty much the same. I worked for the Box M all last winter but me and the foreman never did see eye to eye, so when spring got here I drawed my time. Since then I've just been riding the grub line keeping my eyes open. Then this fellow showed up wanting to get some guys who knew one end of a hammer from the other."

"What is that thing they are building in there?'

"I don't know for sure. It's a wagon. I don't know how a team is gonna be able to pull it the thing must weigh a ton."

"What would you haul in a wagon weighing a ton, feathers?"

Laughing Ed said, "That's about all you could haul in a wagon that heavy. Why would you need a wagon weighing a ton to haul feathers?"

"What makes it so heavy?"

"It's just made out of real heavy material. The walls are three or four inches thick."

"I wonder why they would make it so heavy."

"Beats me, it don't make no sense."

Three nights later Jud and his boys made a quick sweep of the range and gathered up about two-hundred head of cattle. "

"Boys let's drive'em up there and get 'em in the pens. Before anybody can see the brands. Once they are all jammed together in those pens, it'll be pretty near impossible for anybody to read brands."

Jud rode up front and approached one of Grady's men and said, "I've got about two-hundred head that needs to go out on the next train."

"Sir, do you have an appointment to ship today?"

"No I ain't got no appointment. Just get that damn gate open and let me get these critters in the pens. What time is the next train pulling cattle cars due in?"

"Wait just a minute let me go get my boss. I'll be right back."

"Go get 'im maybe he's got sense enough to open the gate when you got cows ready to ship standing right here."

Jud turned around and told his men, "people are stupid you've gotta tell'em what to do."

He turned back around and Grady McCain was standing there. "What're you doing here?"

"Do you want to ship some cattle?"

"Yeah, what's it to you?" Jud asked.

"I own these pens and you're not going to ship anything out of here unless I say so."

"Huh, I thought the railroad owned these pens."

"No, they do not Colleen and I own these pens. Before you ship one cow out of them I'm going to inspect those brands and if I find any altered brands I'm going to send one of the boys for the sheriff."

"You smart mouth punk. There ain't no altered brands. I bought ever head all legal."

"Then you can show me a bill of sale for every cow not wearing the **H-V** brand. As soon as the bills of sale have been verified I'll open the gate. It'll cost you $1.00 per cow to ship them from here."

Grady was looking right at Jud but out of the corner of his eye he was watching a salty looking gun fighter on his left. The man spoke up and said, "Jud, I ain't letting no tender-foot tell me what I can and can't do." He reached for his gun.

Fourteen inches of lead and smoke shot out of the end of Grady's forty-four. Before the gun man's gun cleared leather.

Pointing the forty-four at nobody in particular Grady said, "Does anybody else want to argue about my right to say who ships and who doesn't ship out of my pens and loading chutes?"

Nobody moved.

"That's good. Now let me see those bill-of –sales."

Jud said, "I didn't know I was gonna need 'em so I left them at the ranch house."

Grady motioned with his six –shooter, "let's you and me mosey through this herd and see what brands we have." Dropping the gun back in the holster. They all knew how fast he could get it back out so it didn't make anybody feel any more secure.

Jud said, "Well now most of these are off the **H-V** and you know I own that brand."

"Yes, you do."

When the count was done there was four different brands mixed together. Only thirty-two head wore the **H-V** brand. Grady said, "Jud you can ship thirty-two head wearing the H-V brand. If you show back up here with a bill-of-sale for the other one hundred and sixty five you can ship them too."

Jud stammered and said, "One of these days somebody is gonna take you down a notch or two."

"You tried twice before. How did that work out for you?"

Jud reached back and put his hand on the butt of his gun. Grady calmly said "Don't even think about it. I'll keep those other steers in the corral until train time. If you are not back here with legitimate bills-of-sale. I'm going to drive them back out on the range and turn them lose."

Jud jerked his horses head around and pounded his spurs into the startled animal's side.

Grady looked at the other two and said, "Pick him up and take him with you," pointing to the one on the ground.

One of them snarled, "It's not my job to pick up your trash."

"You have two choices, all you have to do is choose one. Either you pick up your pardner and ride out of here, or you can join him down on the ground."

Both men climbed down off their horses and picked up the would-be gun fighter and tied him across his saddle.

CHAPTER FIFTY-TWO

Jud went to the Wells-Fargo office and collected the money from the sale of his cows. "$540.00 is that all I get for my herd?"

"Sir they brought $17.00 a head, and there is a $14.00 fee for transferring the money so that leaves $540.00. If you would like I'll take time to refigure it for you."

"Just give me the damn money. It's that Grady dude. He's gonna get his one of these days. I've about had it with that meddler. "

Grady happened to walk in and heard Jud's outburst. He said, "Well Jud I'm right here. Turn around and make your play right now."

Jud jerked like he had been hit with a bull nettle. His eyes went wide then he meekly scooped the bills off the counter and said, "Not now but someday."

"Jud, you best keep your mouth shut. One of these days I'm going to call the dance for you. Furthermore I don't want to see you trying to ship any more cattle through my pens. I don't care if they all have **H-V** brands on 'em."

⊨⊨ ⊨⊨

Marlene and Colleen had the catalog open to home furnishing. "Oh Colleen look at this gorgeous armoire, it will look lovely in your bedroom."

"Look at this divan. Wow, look at these draperies. Marlene is this for real. I'll keep thinking I am going to wake up and find I've been dreaming."

"Colleen, just think only a few weeks ago we were homeless. With no means of support. Now look at you."

"I know Grady is the best partner in the world. That man works incredibly hard. You and he are going to have a great life together."

"I just wish I didn't need to go back and finish this year at school. That is going to be hard. I thought I was going to die watching him in that fight. Don't you dare let that man get into anything like that while I'm gone."

"Don't worry. I'll keep an eye on Mr. Grady McCain, after all he's my number one mule skinner." They both laughed.

"Let's make up an order for these things and take it back to the mercantile and get them to order 'em for us."

"It'll be good practice for me to help you decorate this house. Then when I get back and Grady and I get married, you can help me decorate my new house."

"You've got a deal little sister, get your bonnet on, let's go."

CHAPTER FIFTY-THREE

Good morning sheriff." Have you heard or seen anything new on our boy Jud?"

"I sent a letter back to the US marshal. It would be great if we could someway help them get him, at least he would be out of our hair. I guess you heard he tried to ship a bunch of cattle with other people's brands on 'em."

"What happened?"

"Grady wouldn't let him ship anything that didn't have the **H-V** brand on it. Then one of his gunmen tried to pull a sneak shot at Grady and got himself blowed out of the saddle."

"According to what Jacob tells me that boy is quick. I'm glad he's on our side. I don't want to see that US marshal come and get Jud. I want to prove he sneaked into an old man's bed room and murdered him in cold blood with a pillow over his face."

"That was the nastiest, low-down-dirty thing I have ever seen in my life. The man was old, he was partially paralyzed and he left two fine young women alone in this world. "

"Yeah, I'd like to see the dude that did it dancin' on the end of a rope, myself."

"I went back and talked to everybody in town, I even talked to Lizzie again. So far I haven't got anything except I did learn there is a drummer that calls on the mercantile once a month and he was playing cards with Jud the night the murder happened. He's due back in a few day. Maybe he can shed some new light on what happened that night.

"Well Jud only has two gunmen left. Maybe we'll wait a little while and Grady will get rid of all of them for us."

"He's cleaning 'em out pretty fast. I've still got three here in jail. The judge should get here pretty soon and we'll pack them off to the territorial prison. I keep tellin' them that I'll talk to the judge for'em if they'll tell me all they can about Jud's involvement. So far they're being tight lipped. Although the closer it gets to the day the judge is due here the more nervous one of them's getting"

"Say, why you don't send their names and descriptions up to the US marshal. It's possible he may be looking for some of them for something else."

"Now marshal that's a good idea. If I got back a note saying they was wanted in Colorado or somewhere. I'll tell them that'll guarantee the judge will order them hung. They won't know it's hardly ever done anymore. If I can convince them the judge almost always hangs men, if he thinks they're habitual criminals. That might loosen somebody's tongue."

"Especially if one of them could say he was with Jud when he shot that Whitely fellow. Remember his wife said her husband did nothing to provoke getting shot."

"That would get a rope around his neck for sure."

***

Colleen and Marlene walked into Grady's new apartment. "My goodness he may as well have stayed in the hay loft. He doesn't even have a bed. Look he's sleeping on a blanket on the floor and his clothes are piled over in the corner. We've got to go get the man some fixins."

"Yes, he needs a bed, a chest of drawers and a shift-robe," Marlene said.

"Well he also needs plates, cups, pans and an iron skillet. At least he's got a stove."

Laughing Marlene said, "If I 'm going to marry the man I see right now he's going to take some domesticating."

"He has gone with one of the wagons so let's get one of the drivers to go with us and buy what he needs. He'll be surprised when he gets home, we'll have turned this box in the corner of a warehouse into a livable apartment."

"Before we do that let me get my Bible and let's bless this place where Grady is going to live." Colleen reached into her reticule and pulled out her Bible. She thumbed through it and stopped on the book of Numbers chapter six and ran her finger down to the twenty-fourth verse, *And the LORD spake unto Moses, saying, , On this wise ye shall bless the people, The LORD bless thee, and keep thee: The LORD make his face shine upon thee, and be gracious unto thee:*

"Lord that is our prayer for Grady, we ask for your blessing on him and all who enter into this home."

In Jesus name,

Amen

CHAPTER FIFTY-FOUR

Grady walked around looking at the heavy wagon and said, "How long will it be before someone realizes what this wagon is for?"

Ronnie and Lonnie both looked at each other and Ronnie said, "If I'm the one driving it I hope they never find out."

"That's why we are keeping it out if sight here in the warehouse. We don't want anybody even speculating about what it might be hauling."

Lonnie said, "That ain't likely. You haven't even told us."

"No I haven't and I'm not going to until that train gets here. I trust you two completely, but as long as I haven't told even you there's no chance that someone could over hear our conversation."

"Can I ask who the shipper is?"

"It's the US government."

After Grady walked away Ronnie said, "I'll bet its some new gun for the fort."

"Unless it is a new cannon I can't imagine why the wagon would need to be so strong. Look at them side boards they are four inches thick."

"Everything about this wagon is strange look how tall the side boards are. The driver is sitting down in the box. I sat on that seat the other day and my head was barely over the top. In fact if you look the reins are going to run through the front of the wagon. I ain't never seen a wagon built like that."

"Maybe it's gonna haul one of the new Gatling guns. You know they could mount it in the back of the wagon. You know the Indians ain't got nothing that will shoot through those side boards."

"I don't know what it is but they sure are making a big deal of keeping it secret. What else could the US government be shipping besides something for the fort?"

Jud walked into the saloon and met his two new associates that worked out at Grady's warehouse. "How did things go today?"

"Just about through with this job. When are you gonna let us in on what you're planning?"

"What did you find out about that mysterious wagon?"

"Not much, one of the guys working on the dock over heard two railroad engineers talking about something coming in on a train from the US government."

"What could the government be shipping that would be so heavy they would need a special heavy duty wagon to haul it?"

"That's a funny thing. The floor boards are regular thickness. It's the side walls that are extra thick. The wheels are taller and wider."

The other man said, "Everything about that wagon is strange. The driver sits down in the box his head is barely above the side-boards and the reins run through the front. I ain't never seen a wagon like that."

"Do you see ole Grady around there much?"

"Not much he's in and out."

"I hate that arrogant man. He thinks he's a big shot. Ever since him and that O'Shanity gal bought their first wagon it seems luck just follows him around. I aim to bring him back down. He killed two of my men. I need you two boys to keep working out there as long as you can. I have a hunch there is going to be a lot of money to be made on whatever it is they are planning to ship in that wagon. We need to find out what it is and where it's going."

"You planning on stealing it?"

"I'm going to destroy everything Grady McCain has built then I'm gonna kill him. If you 've got the stomach for a fight, I'll cut you in as soon as we know what they are bringing in and when."

Later that evening Jud sat in the kitchen with a bottle of whiskey. "You two guys have stuck by me and I'm gonna make it good for you. Out there at the depot, they have a special wagon in that warehouse. It's all secret.

CHAPTER FIFTY-FIVE

Every minute he was not working, Grady spent with Marlene.
"Grady, are you sure we are doing the right thing?"

"Darling you know it is. I'll scout around and find us a great piece of land and I'll build us a new house just like the plans you and I drew up. When you get back your husband and your new home will be waiting for you."

Marlene kissed him and said, "Oh Grady, I miss you already."

"I probably won't even think about you. I'll be so busy running the business and building a new house."

"You better be busy writing me a new letter every day. Because if I go a whole week without a letter from you Mr. McCain. I will drop out of school and catch the very next train back to Texas. That's a promise."

Laughing Grady said, "You would too. Golly at two cents a letter I'd go broke buying stamps."

She reached into her receptacle pulled out a silver dollar and said, "I'll pay for the first fifty stamps," Laughing she said, "but you better find another dollar before these stamps run out."

Three weeks later Grady said, "Darling it's time to go," He picked up her last bag and placed it in the back of the buggy. Then lifted her up to the seat. Marlene took out a handkerchief and started to dry her eyes.

"Sweetheart, this year will be over before you know it. Just remember we are doing this to honor your, father. He gave his all for you to have this opportunity."

She sobbed, "I know, I just never thought it would be this hard."

Colleen came out of the house and Grady lifted her up in the back seat next to Marlene. It looks like the queen and her court as he climbed in the driver's seat beside Knot.

When they arrived at the depot Grady tenderly lifted Marlene out of the buggy, then helped Colleen down to the platform. As the two sisters hugged, he pulled her luggage from the buggy and handed them to the porter. Then Marlene was in his arms. He gently kissed her, and whispered, "good bye my darling. I will write every day."

Marlene wiped her eyes and said, "You know what will happen of you don't."

The next thing he knew he was watching the back of the train disappear over the horizon in the east. He swallowed hard several times then said, "Well partner, I've got to find some land and start building a house."

"Grady, how are we doing out here? Are we going to be ready when that shipment arrives?"

"The special wagon is finished, do you want to see it?"

"Yes, I would like to see that thing we have been talking about for so long."

"Colleen, it's only been a few weeks."

"Well it seems like we have been talking about that wagon for a long time."

Grady opened the door to the warehouse and they stepped in.

"From here it looks like all of the other wagons except its green."

"Wait until you get closer."

"Oh my goodness. That thing must weigh a ton."

"It probably does."

"How can a team pull that thing with any weight in the wagon?"

"A team couldn't, that is why I'm using a six horse hitch. Except it will be six of our best draft mules."

"Why're the side boards six inches think?"

"They are actually four and a half inches thick they are two, two inch pine boards sandwiched together with a hard as iron sheet of dried buffalo hide in between. No bullet should shoot through them."

"Are you planning to ride with the cargo yourself?"

"Yes. I'll have Lonnie driving, with me, Ronnie and Milt in the back with Winchesters."

"Grady, are you sure that's a good idea. You know Marlene wouldn't want you to ride in that thing if there was a chance of it getting attacked."

"Colleen, you know I can't ask other men to do something that I won't do myself. With any luck we'll get the cargo delivered before anybody even knows what we're hauling so there'll be no reason to attack a simple freight wagon."

CHAPTER FIFTY-SIX

J ud was playing poker in the saloon with a man who worked at the bank. Just making conversation Jud asked, "How are things in the banking business?"

"It's fixing to get really good with this new thing the federal government is fixing to do."

"Oh, what's that?'

"Well we're really not supposed to talk about it but since you are not in the banking business, I guess I can tell you. Our bank is one of twenty banks that have been selected to try a new experiment that's supposed to stimulate the economy."

"How do you stimulate an economy?"

"Well the theory is the US government will loan twenty banks in one region $10,000.00 cash and they in turn are to loan it out to ranchers and business men to help them grow bigger and hire more people."

Jud's mind was whirling. *Twenty banks times $10,000.00, wow, that's $200,000.00. If one man got hold of that kind of money he could own the world. A special wagon to haul two hundred thousand in gold. Is that possible?*

He lost the next hand on purpose and said, "I feel my luck is starting to run bad. I better quit. I'll see you next time."

He walked over to the two men who worked for Grady and said, "Have you ever figured out what they are planning to haul in that special wagon?"

"No they're being tight lipped about that wagon. Still have never brought it out of the warehouse."

"Tell me again what is special about that wagon?"

"Well I got in there the other day and from a distance it looks just like all of the other wagons except its painted green, and the wheels are bigger and wider. When you get up close the side boards are about six inches thick. But the floor is just like all the other wagons and the driver's seat is not up on top so he can see where he's going. The driver sits down almost on the floor. His head is barely above the front of the freight box. Another funny thing the reins are fed through the front of the box. It's strange. I wouldn't want to drive that thing you couldn't see where you was goin'."

"Other than the thickness of the side board is there anything else unusual about that wagon?"

"Well the big wheels and another thing the sideboards are taller than normal."

"What do you mean by taller?"

"You know a normal freight wagon's sideboards are about three feet tall. These are about four and a half feet tall. Another thing that's strange is all the way around the top of the sideboard every few feet they've got port holes cut in the sideboard."

That is strange. Why would they beef up the side walls and not beef up the floor, if they were hauling gold it's heavy. You would think the floor would need to be strengthened. That would explain the big wheels wider wouldn't sink down in the dirt and bigger could roll over stuff.

"There's another thing that's strange,"

"What's that?"

"They're rigging it for a six horse hitch. They'll be using mules instead of horses but they'll have six mules pulling that wagon."

An overweight wagon pulled by six mules. Okay six mules makes sense. It is heavy and hauling a heavy load. Why didn't they beef up the floor like they did the sideboards?

"Mr. Rawlins, you said you was gonna let us in on something, if we help ya. Well we've done about all we can. Cause tomorrow is our last day to work out there. The foreman told us today that tomorrow was our last day. We are through building ever thang they wanted built."

"I'll tell you what. When you get through tomorrow don't come here. I want y'all to meet me out at the ranch. I'm gonna introduce you to a couple of more men and we'll all sit down and talk about how to get richer than you ever dreamed about. Keep your eyes and ears open tomorrow and see if you can find out when they are planning to bring out that green wagon."

CHAPTER FIFTY-SEVEN

The marshal walked into the sheriff's office. "They said you wanted to see me. What-cha got?"

"Remember you said, we should look some more into our boys back trail?"

"Yeah."

"I got back in touch with that US Marshal and he didn't have anything else to add. Then I remembered I knew the town marshal there in Denver City. So I contacted him. Here's the letter I got back from him." He handed a letter to the marshal.

The marshal started to read it and his eye brows went up. He let out a low whistle. It says here that the woman he's thought to have killed was smothered with a pillow while she slept."

"That's why I sent for ya. What should we do next?"

They were both quiet for a minute thinking then the marshal said, "Why don't you come with me and let's go back over to the doc's house and go over the crime scene again with a fine tooth comb. If we could find anything that would prove he was there other than that chain link we've got'im."

"If we don't find anything there what else can we do? We have a motive even though his lawyer will say it's not. We have another murder in another territory that was done in the same way by a man who meets his description. A good lawyer will get him off sure as shootin' if we try him with no more than what we've got so far."

"I know but it sure sticks in my craw. I know he's as guilty as sin."

The sheriff twirled his handle bar mustache then said, "Have you been out by the Hill-Valley ranch lately?"

"Naw, I haven't been out that way for a while. Why?"

"Remember how well kept the property was as long as O'Shanity owned it?"

"Yeah, it was one of the nicest places around here," the marshal said.

"It ain't no more. It is a raw hide looking place now. All growed up in weeds around the house. One of the barn doors is hanging loose, some of the rails on the corral are busted. It's pitiful."

"When a man builds it himself he'll take care of it. Jud ain't built nothing."

"I don't know about you but I'm gonna put every man I've got out digging for something I can pin on Jud Rawlins. I want something that will put him in that house on that night." The marshal said.

"You go after him from that angle and I'll keep digging on his back trail. Let me know if you find anything. I want to be there when we strap the irons on that dude," the sheriff said.

"I will and you let me know if anything shows up."

The railroad men stepped off the westbound train and walked into the one room depot. Grady was waiting for them. "Good morning Grady. Thanks for meeting us. How are you coming with getting the wagon and teams together?

"Come on I'll show you." They walked into the warehouse and there sat the completed wagon. "I have six of my best draft mules in the corral out back. I've got my most trusted two men driving and I'm personally going to be riding in the back. In fact I'm going to have three of us with repeating rifles riding in the wagon."

"Have you heard any rumors about what you're going to be hauling?"

"No, I haven't heard any. One reason, I haven't told anyone not even the men who are going to be driving or riding shot gun. I think there is some speculation about what it could be, but so far the speculation seems to be more toward a new shipment of guns and ammunition for the army post."

"Grady you were smart to keep this wagon out of sight. It is bound to cause some gossip."

"When is the shipment due to arrive?"

"They are waiting for us to send back a report saying you have everything ready on this end."

"I believe we're as ready as we can get."

"Here is the way it's supposed to go down, the shipment will arrive on the morning train. The cargo will be packed in plain wooden boxes. You are to pull your wagon up beside the baggage car and they will off load the boxes right into the wagon. You'll have a list of all the recipients and you are to go directly to the first bank without delay and drop off two boxes. Then proceed directly to the next. Until they are all safely delivered."

"Who has been guarding it all the way to here?"

"The railroad has a dozen of the best security people riding with it to here."

"I talked to the sheriff and he's going to have two deputies riding with us and I'll have four Winchesters in the wagon. I wonder if that's enough."

"If the security has held and nobody knows what we are hauling we should be okay. If we put too many guns riding with the wagon it will bring too much attention. I'm not even sure we should have the two deputy's escorting you."

"If anybody happens to notice all they'll see is forty small boxes loaded on a wagon. It could be groceries for all they know."

CHAPTER FIFTY-EIGHT

Marlene sat down in her room at school and opened the first letter from Grady. A smile spread across her face as she recognized the hand writing.

My Dearest Marlene,

My days are filled with work and my nights are filed with dreams of when you will be back in my arms. Forever.

I found a beautiful piece of ground. It is just one mile south of town, there is a spring fed creek running through it and some large pecan trees where I want to build the house. I will situate the house so the trees shade the front porch. You will love it. The view from the front porch is very good. Standing there I was looking at the most spectacular site. All of the sage were in full bloom. The whole hillside was draped in royal purple sage. I thought, perfect for a queen.

I hope you packed enough warm clothing for winter. I understand Boston has pretty rough winters. I don't want my princess to freeze.

Honey I miss you more than I thought I would. We did the right thing. I hope Mr. O'Shanity can see what his little girl is doing to honor him.

I am counting the days until you are in my arms for good.

With all my love,
Grady

She immediately picked up a pen and wrote.

Grady Darling,

If you had told me it was going to be this hard I would never have come.

It was a beautiful thought when you said you hoped my daddy was looking down at what we are doing. I received a letter today from you and one from Colleen.

I understand from her letter that the special shipment you have been expecting is to arrive soon. She also tells me you are planning to ride with it.

That terrifies me. Please be careful. I couldn't stand it, if something happened to you. You are the wind in my breath. Without you I would cease to breathe.

Could you get someone to make a drawing that will show where the house will sit and what the house will look like? I know we together decided how the house was to be built and where each room will be but I can't imagine what the house would look like. I know it will be beautiful and we'll live in it and raise a family in it. That house is going to be a house of love. Because love is building it.

I must close now I have school work to do. It seems so childish to be here at school when there is so much going on there.

You are my love, my life.
Marlene XOXO

CHAPTER FIFTY-NINE

Jud asked "What would they be hauling in a wagon with a normal floor but super strong sides. Why would the driver be sitting down in the box instead of up on a normal seat? Why would they build a wagon so strong and heavy it would take six mules to pull it? Yet not reinforce the floor?"

"They say them sideboards are six inches thick. Even a Winchester won't go through it," one of the other guys said.

"Why all the secrecy?"

"Whatever it is, it must be light and valuable."

Jud snapped his fingers, "they are going to be hauling cash money. I thought it was gold but this is even better. They are going to be hauling regular old US money to the banks in that wagon."

"Why is paper money better than gold Jud?'

"Because you can spend it anywhere and it weighs a lot less than gold. Hot damn, we've got to figure out when it's gonna get here and which way they are going to be heading out to make the deliveries. If we can get to them before they get to the first bank we can ride off with all $200,000.00 in cash money. Guys we can go to California or back east and live like gentlemen. I mean with maids and butlers and stuff." *I wonder how I can get rid of these lowlifes and keep it all.*

"How are we gonna split it Jud?"

"I'm gonna take half, cause it's my job. I'm the one who planned it and organized it. You four can split the other hundred between ya. You each'll be richer than you ever dreamed with $25,000.00 in your saddle bags. Which is more money that a normal cowhand would make in his entire life."

"Wait a minute, you plan on taking half and leave us to split the other half?"

"If you've got a problem with that you can leave right now and you will get nothing. What's it gonna be?"

"Oh. Forget it Jud I was just askin'."

"Okay boys here's what we do. You'll slip back into town and hang around. Keep your ears open, see if you can get a hint on when it's coming. I think it's real soon."

"I'll stop by the bank and see if I can get my banker friend to join me in a friendly game of poker. Put a little liquor in him and see if he'll loosen up a little more."

Colleen walked into the lawyer's office, "Good morning Sir."

"Colleen you have an amazing business head on your shoulders. I talked to the sheriff and the judge, they both like your idea. I talked to the town council and they want to get started right away. So we can get it done before the rain starts, how soon can you get started?"

She laughed and said, "I haven't even told Grady yet. Let me get back to you in a few days. We have that special delivery we have to do for the US government, as soon as that is done, we can get started."

"Colleen do you know when it's coming?"
"No not yet. But soon. Everything is ready on our end."

Grady sat down and pulled off his boots, and said, "Knot old buddy what's the matter? You feeling a little off your feed. You 've been moping around the last few days." He reached down and scratched the dog's ears the tail went to wagging. "That's more like it let's get some sleep."

He laid down in the bed and looked over at Knot curled up on the floor and said, "You know winters is coming pretty soon. I'm gonna build you a bed. I've got enough scrap lumber left from all this construction we did around here. I can hammer you a bed together then get a quilt and fold it in the bottom. Then you'll be just fine all winter."

Then he thought I didn't write my letter today so he got back out of bed and went to his desk.

My dearest Marlene,

Things are going great here. The deal is done on the land and I have a contractor lined up for the house. I told him he would build the house but the finishing touches, like the paint for the walls would have to wait until you were here. I can do the rough stuff but the petty stuff was your department.

My love I miss you so much, it's pretty lonesome here every night talking to Knot. That dog just ain't got a lot to say. I 'm sorta worried about old Knot. I have no idea how old Knot is. Knot was full grown when he found me that night. Anyway old Knot just hasn't acted like Knot the last few days. I don't know what's wrong.

Anyway me and old Knot both miss you. I am waiting for your sister to drop something new on me any day now.

The first four thousand head of cattle are due here in the morning. The special shipment we talked about is coming soon. The freight wagons are staying busy. We are running six to eight wagons a day now.

Marlene my love my arms ache to hold you. I can't wait until Christmas so I can see you again.

All my love,
Grady

CHAPTER SIXTY

Jud met the banker at the saloon and brought a bottle over to the table. "

"Tonight I'm feeling lucky I hope you brought your rabbit's foot with you."

The young man who worked at the bank laughed and said, "Jud if you don't play any better tonight than you did the last time we played I won't need any rabbit's foot." He felt very comfortable with his new friend. Jud was a lot more fun to be around than that crotchety old banker he worked with all day.

They played and Jud let the boy win when the pot was small. Being careful not to get greedy. He kept refilling the young man's whiskey glass. Finally he said, "When is this big new deal with the banks going to go down?"

"We're not supposed to talk about that."

"I know but I've been a little worried ever since we talked about it last time. I just need to know when to pull my money out of the bank before something happens to the bank. Maybe the government is gonna shut'em down or something."

The young man sorta slurred his words when he said, "Ohhh noos nothin' like that. Your money issh gonna, be even more safe on Wednesday mornin' than it is today. That's all I gotta say."

They played a couple of more hands and Jud lost so he said, "Darn, I guess I wasn't feeling so lucky after all. We better call it a night I 've got a busy day ahead of me tomorrow."

The next morning Jud strutted into the kitchen, "What did you boys learn?"

"I did learn one thing. Grady had the mules out working them in a six-horse-hitch looked like he was getting them used to it."

"I learned it is going down next Wednesday morning." Jud said, "I figure the shipment is going to be on that west bound train early Wednesday morning. They'll probably off load it right on to that special wagon they built and head for the nearest bank. That's right here in town, so we can't do much between the rail and the first bank but we'll watch and see which way they go when they leave there. We can ride a lot faster than that heavy wagon can go so we'll head 'em off before they get there.

Here's the thing boys thit's a huge amount of money. We're gonna have everybody including the US army after us. If they catch us we'll hang for sure. If they don't we'll live like kings. When we stop that wagon we can't leave any witnesses behind that can put a finger on anyone of us. If you've got a problem with that you need to get out now but keep your mouth shut don't betray the rest of us."

One of the new men said, "How much did you say my part would be?"

"About $25,000.00."

"I'd have to punch cows for seventy years to make that much."

CHAPTER SIXTY-ONE

The next day Grady stopped by the house, Colleen said, "Are you worried about somebody trying to hold up the wagon hauling all that money?"

"If they find out about it, you can guarantee it. For that much money the Mexican government might send Santa Anna."

Late that evening, Grady was walking from the loading chutes back toward the warehouse after watching the last of the four thousand steers loaded on the train. When he felt a hand hit him in the chest and knock him back, just as a high powered bullet split the air right in front of his face. He ducked down and whipped out his gun in time to see a rider streaking away on a mouse colored horse.

Grady was stunned. Who tried to shoot me? Who was it that pushed me out of the way? He looked around and there was no one there except him and Knot.

Grady said, "Knot did you push me? You're the only other living thing I see out here." Still puzzled by it all he walked into the apartment. Knot went immediately and curled up in the bed Grady had made.

Colleen sat down and was totaling up her books. She said "Lord you have really blessed us with so much success. A few weeks ago Marlene and I were two homeless women. Now I have a beautiful home, a strong business partner, and Marlene has a fiancé who loves her dearly. Then she thought about what the pastor had said about paying tithes. He quoted a scripture in Malachi. She reached for her Bible and found Malachi and thumbed through it until she found the eighth verse it read:

"Will a man rob God? Yet you are robbing Me! But you say, 'How have we robbed You?' In tithes and offerings. 9 "You are cursed with a curse, for you are robbing Me, the whole nation of you! 10 "Bring the whole tithe into the storehouse, so that there may be food in My house, and test Me now in this," says the LORD of hosts, "if I will not open for you the windows of heaven and pour out for you a blessing until it overflows.

Colleen said, "Oh God I am so sorry, you are blessing me and I have not been doing my part. Please forgive me. As for my half of the business I pledge to you right now. I will start giving one tenth of everything I make to you. Lord I can't speak for Grady, but I will speak to him and tell him what I am doing. I will show him the verse in Malachi."

She sat down and wrote a letter to Marlene.

Jud said, "Here is the plan boys. We know it's going down Wednesday morning. It stands to reason that the bank here in town will be the first delivery. There is only four roads leading out of town. So here's what I want you to do. Each one of you take a road and go the way that wagon will have to go. Search for a place where we can ambush it."

"How're we gonna ambush it if the walls are six inches thick no bullet will go through that?"

"I've thought of that. First we'll get some bows and arrows from the Indians. We'll kill the mules. When they're stopped we'll start lobbing flaming arrows into the wagon. It's made of varnished wood. It may be bullet proof but it ain't fire proof. It'll burn quick when we get a few flaming arrows into it. When those inside the wagon come out we'll mow 'em down and grab the cash before the fire can get to it and we'll be gone. With any luck everybody will think the Indians did it when they see them arrows. By the time they figure out it wasn't the Indians, we'll be on a train for the east or a ship for the orient or wherever else you've always hankered to see. My advice to you is go to the nearest railroad and catch a train clean out of this country. If you hang around they will sooner or later catch you and you will hang."

Grady was still a little rattled after his near miss with the grim reaper and a little worried about Knot. He sat down and picked up his Bible. He had not looked at it since he left the boys home. In there he was required to read it ever day. But out here on his own it just didn't happen. When he laid it on his lap it fell open to Malachi chapter three, when he got down to verse eight he remembered the pastor's sermon. He read it again then he said, "*Lord I am sorry. I have sinned. You have blessed me more than any young man on earth. You brought me from sleeping in a barn to owning half interest in a thriving business and you brought me the smartest partner a man could have, and most of all you brought me Marlene.*

Lord you blessed me first and I have not been bringing my tithe to your house. Father I cannot speak for Colleen but right now I pledge to give ten percent of every dollar I make out of the this business to your work. I will speak to Colleen and tell her what I want to do with my half of the profits.

While I am talking to you Lord bless old Knot, I know Knot is just a dog but a good dog and I ask you to bless my dog."

Amen

———

The deputy walked into the marshal's office, "Did you hear that somebody tried to ambush Grady last night as he walked from the loading chute back to his apartment in that new warehouse building?"

"No, what happened?"

"Apparently somebody laid for him with a high powered rile and as he was walking back to his apartment, somebody took a shot at him just before Sundown only missed by a whisker of taking him out."

"Did anybody see anything?"

"Grady saw the back of a man on a grey horse racing away but the sun was in Grady's eyes so he couldn't see much."

"You know we never had these problems until Jud Rawlins came here."

"Do you want me to go get him and bring him in for questioning?"

"No that slimy lawyer will have him out in five minutes. I want you guys to find me something or someone who will put him at the doc's house the night Mr. O'Shanity was murdered."

CHAPTER SIXTY-TWO

The railroad men walked in to Grady's apartment because the door was standing open. "Good morning Grady, you got a minute?"

Grady was going over his driver schedule, He looked up, and said, "Sure come on in. Have we got a firm date for that delivery?"

"Yes, next Wednesday on the early morning train. Here is the list of banks that we are to deliver to. I assume you'll start with the one here in town."

"Let me study the list. I'll route them using the knowledge we've got of the terrain and distance."

"Have you had any reason to think anybody has found out what you'll be hauling?"

"No I'm not too worried about this one but every one after this is going to be a concern."

"Well one thing we can do, is we can vary the delivery dates so they won't always come on the same day each month."

"That'll help some. I sure don't want to get one of my drivers killed hauling somebody else's money."

"No and we don't want to get anybody killed either. We also don't want to lose a bunch of Uncle Sam's money."

"Let's get this one behind us and then we'll worry about another one."

"Well Grady, we'll let you finish your work. We're going to meet the bankers and make sure everything is ready on their end."

As they were leaving the younger man hung back and said, "I asked Miss O'Shanity if I could call on her. She said since her father was dead I should ask you."

Grady looked up and grinned, "She did, did she? Let me tell you something. As you know I'm engaged to Colleen's sister. Colleen and I were partners before I was engaged to her sister. I told her that since Marlene's father was dead I guessed I should ask her for permission to court her sister. She said yes I should ask her and she wanted me to get on with it. So I guess she thinks it only fair that I give my permission for someone to call on her. If you are an honorable man you have my blessing, if you are not I'll hunt you down." Grady stood and stuck out his hand, "Good luck , that sister in law of mine is a real thoroughbred, you will be in for a ride. Just remember what I said she may be my sister- in- law but she is more like my sister and she owns half of this company, don't make me come looking for you."

"Oh no sir. Thank you sir. I better catch my partner." He grabbed his hat and ran out the door.

Grady looked after the man and thought, *good lord, I'm no older that he is but I feel so old.*

Sunday morning Grady stopped by the house to pick op Colleen. As he lifted her up into the carriage he said, "What's the idea of telling that young man he needed my permission to court you?"

"Well since you are almost my brothel-in-law I figured you were the one responsible for giving men permission to call on me, besides you owed me for giving you permission to call on Marlene. "

"That I do. If you remember you almost ordered me to call on Marlene."

"Grady McCain, I did not."

"Well even if you didn't you should have."

"Well what did you tell Cliff?"

"Is that his name? His knees was knocking so loud if he said his name I didn't hear it."

"You are impossible what did you tell the man?"

"I told him I wished him good luck because if he thought he could keep up with you he was in for one heck of a ride. "

She whacked him over shoulder with her umbrella and said, "You didn't tell him that."

"Yes I did. I also told him he had better be a man of honor because if he wasn't I'd come looking for him and he didn't want me looking for him."

She had a horrified look on her face, "Did you really tell him that?"

"Yes I did,"

"Oh Grady, he was really nice and you probably scared the poor man off."

"Do you really think somebody telling me something like that would have kept me from courting Marlene?"

"No, but you are different."

"Colleen, if he is a real man he will not be frightened off by me saying that. If his intentions are not honorable he better move on because I wasn't kidding. "

"I don't know whether to hug you or whack you with this umbrella again."

Grady stopped the carriage, and said, "Oh there is something I need to tell you."

"What."

"I've been thinking about the pastor's sermon about tithing so I looked up the passage in Malachi and reread it. "I promised God that I was going to start paying the tithes from my half of the money."

Colleen's eyes lit up, "Grady I was going to tell you that I had decided to pay tithes on my half of the money."

"Really, you know in Malachi it says God will pour out blessing after you tithe, in our case he did his part first."

CHAPTER SIXTY-THREE

Monday morning the lawyer came by the house on Hickory Street and tapped on the door. Colleen came to the door. "Oh hello Mr. Thacker, please come in. I was getting ready to have a fresh cup of coffee would you like one?"

She said over her shoulder, "Mandy bring two please."

"I didn't know you had servants."

"Oh no, Mandy and her husband Hershel are like family. Grady hired her to help with the house. Hershel needed a job and I needed some help with the things outside the house, so I hired him. Grady's keeping me so busy keeping up with all the books. I didn't have time to clean this house. So Grady took it upon himself to hire someone to help me. I threatened to get a gun and shoot him but after I met Mandy, I think she was sent by God and then I found out her husband was looking for work too. It was a miracle."

"What does he do?"

"Well I've got my own carriage and a beautiful black filly named Dolly. He takes care of Dolly and when I want to go somewhere he harnesses her up for me. He keeps the weeds cut and the trees trimmed. He is just an angel. If I need something I tell Mandy and she tells him."

"Well Colleen, I will admit you and Grady handle success more graciously than most. I stopped by because the council wants to know when you can start on that street project."

"We just found out that the shipment will be here Wednesday morning so once that delivery has been made we can start the next day if it's alright with the Sheriff."

Jud and his team met at the edge of town and each one took a different road out of town. Jud went by the bank to say hello to his new friend.

When he walked in there were no customers, "Good morning, got time to shoot the bull a minute?"

"Oh sure, as you can see we don't have any other customers and the old skin flint has gone to get his morning coffee. What –cha got on your mind?"

"Aw, nothing in particular. I'm still a little bit worried about my money being in the bank when I know something is going down and I don't know what it is."

The bank employee leaned in a little closer and whispered, "I told you not to worry. Wednesday morning we are getting a new infusion of working capital to use as loans to local business people. We will be the first bank in the area but they are all getting the same amount. "

"Well congratulations. I wonder who the number two bank in the area is if you guys are number one?"

He looked around to make sure no one else was in the bank and said, "Beard."

Jud left the bank shortly thereafter and met his men coming back from their rides. "I've got it, they're going to Beard when they leave here. Let's ride east and find a place for an ambush."

A few miles east of town Jud pulled up and said. "This looks good. They'll be going slow when they come up out of that dry creek bed. There's plenty of brush and stuff we can hide in. We can build a fire up under those cedars so the smoke will spread out as it drifts up through those thick branches so they won't see it."

"Where do you want us to be?"

"I want two of you on the other side of the road and two of you on this side. One of you shoot the driver, remember he's not sitting up on the seat like a normal driver. It's going to be a head shot 'cause that's all you'll have to shoot at. The rest of you shoot the mules. Bud you take the driver and you two boys on the south side have three mules on your side. Make sure you kill all three.

Little John you get the lead mule on this side. Then both of you shoot the mules on this side. I want all six mules dead. As soon as you hit your target you get down on the ground because those port holes are gun ports. That wagon will start spitting lead like you've never seen before. They'll be shooting in every direction so don't keep standing."

"Where're you going to be?"

"I'm going to be hunkered down behind that little ridge back there behind the cedar trees. As soon as their firing slows down I'll start lobbing flaming arrows into that wagon. Stay down so you don't stop any lead. Keep your eyes on the wagon, as soon as you see those flaming arrows hitting it, they're going to be busy trying to put out the fires. They will be less interested in shooting at you."

"Do we shoot them when they try to jump out of the wagon?"

"Yes, we don't want to leave no witness, kill every one of them, dead men can't testify at no trial if we was to get caught. As soon as they are all down, run like the devil over there and get those crates of money out of the wagon. We don't want to burn up the cash."

"What time's that train supposed to get here?"

"I looked at the posted schedule. The west bound is due in at 6:40 Wednesday morning," looking at his watch he said, "boys in about forty-three hours we'll be the richest men in the territory if not the whole state. Thanks to Uncle Sam and Grady McCain."

⊨⊣ ⊢⊨

The marshal and the sheriff along with four deputies showed up at Doc's house. "Doc I hate to bother you but we want to search that room one more time where Mr. O'Shanity was murdered. I keep thinking we missed some clue. The boys are gonna search all around the yard, me and the sheriff are gonna search that room again from top to bottom."

"You are welcome to look but we sweep and mop the floors every day. We change the bed sheets every time a new person sleeps in that bed. I don't see how you can find anything this late."

CHAPTER SIXTY-FOUR

Grady got up and looked over at Knot. "How're you feeling to-day ole buddy? I just realized I have no idea how old you are." The dog wagged its tail but didn't get up from the bed.

Grady went over to the house on Hickory Street and tapped on the door. Colleen looked up and saw him standing in front of the screen door. "Good morning partner. Come on in. I 'm glad you're here. We need to go over some things."

"Colleen I've been figuring and we need to order three more wagons to make the rock haul work. I simply can't spare three off the freight runs. We'll get too far behind."

"That was one of the things I wanted to talk about. I agree. Why don't you stop over at the freight yard and place an order today?"

"You'll need to give me a bank draft for half of the price so I can put a rush on the order."

She reached into a drawer in her desk and pulled out a bank draft and handed it to him.

"Grady I was planning to go over and pay Mr. Johnson for this month's feed bill. Could you drop it off for me?"

"Yeah, I need to stop by and see that old skin flint anyway. After all this whole freighting idea was his idea. He had the idea and you had the money. I had the strong back, that's worked out to be a good combination so far."

"Have you received a letter from Marlene this week?"

"Got one yesterday. Apparently school is going well. It's getting more into fall up there. She says the trees are beautiful in fall colors."

"Will you be glad when this money is delivered?"

"I'll be honest with you I will be glad. Logically the next few shipments are probably the ones we need to worry most about. But yes I am nervous about this one. I keep going over every detail in my mind I can't think of any way we can be more prepared."

"Have you got the routing figured out?"

"Yes, we'll deliver to the bank here in town first and then head for Beard, then over to Cisco, turn North to Abernathy, just make a big circle back to Abilene. It'll take all day. Won't get to Buffalo Gap before sundown."

"I'm going to spend the day praying for you and the guys. Things are going too good, the last thing we need is for something bad to happen now."

Tuesday drug by, Grady was busy with the freight hauling contracts, but his mind was always on that green wagon. Had he overlooked anything?

It was late in the evening when he drug his weary body back to the apartment. When he walked in Knot was still in the bed, he said, "Knot I wish I knew what to do to make you feel better."

Grady sliced off some bacon and put it in the cast iron skillet. Then took his knife and opened a can of beans. After he ate supper he crawled in it and took a bath in the a metal tub installed in his apartment. Before he climbed into bed he read Marlene's latest letter, then he decided to write a letter back to Marlene.

My Dearest Marlene,

I do not know the words to express to you how much I love you. Everything I write seems trite and inadequate. You have changed my whole world. I did not know this much love even existed until I met you. I love you with all my heart. I am amazed that someone as beautiful and full of life as you would also fall in love with me.

Darling I am counting the days until Colleen and I can come to Boston. But if something should happen to me before I can come I want you to truly know how much I adore you.

I wish I was an artist, I would like to paint a picture of you and your beautiful smile.

Tomorrow we are going on a very unusual and long delivery. I probably will not have an opportunity to write again tomorrow night. Just know this, the last thing I think about every night and the first thing I think about every morning. is my beautiful green eyed girl with flaming red hair.

Good night my love,
Grady

CHAPTER SIXTY-FIVE

Wednesday morning Grady rolled out of bed and threw a stick on the bed of coals in the bottom of his stove. As soon as he had a flame he closed the metal door and placed a coffee pot on the top. Then grabbed the cast iron skillet and sliced some more bacon into it.

After eating breakfast he took down his Winchester and cleaned it and oiled it. Then loaded the magazine full of bullets. Then he took his six-gun and cleaned it and loaded all six bullets in it. He just had a bad feeling about today. He left Marlene's letter on the table so if he didn't make it back Colleen could see that she got it.

He looked over at Knot laying in the dog bed he had made. Well Knot if I make it back tonight and I think, I will I hope you surprise me by looking better when I get back. You take care old friend," he reached down and stroked the dog's head.

Jud said, "Okay boys make sure them guns are cleaned and loaded. We sure don't need no gun to jam during this mêlée."

We're going to mount up here in a little while we've got plenty of time. Roscoe, cook us up some good breakfast, today's a day of celebration. Before this day is over our lives is gonna make a big change."

After breakfast Jud said, "Okay boys let's go over the game plan one more time. We need to, make sure everybody is in-sync, timing is the key to success in this operation."

"Now, Less where are you going to be when the shootin' starts?"

"I'm gonna take a couple of guys and we're gonna be hidin' in the bushes on the south side of the road."

"Okay now everybody listen up. Bud is gonna be on the other side of the road. He's gonna kill the driver with the first shot. We know they're gonna have two deputies riding with them. Little John you and Roy each take one of them deputies. I want the driver and both deputies killed immediately. Don't nobody start shooting until Bud does. The minute you hear Bud's shot open up on the mule, kill both deputies and every animal."

"Jud why do we kill the animals, they can't testify against us."

"We want to make sure that nobody escapes. If them mules are all dead that wagon ain't goin' no where."

"Now Little John where are you going to be when the shooting starts?

"Me and the boys are gonna be here on the north side of the road and we are gonna kill the three mules on this side."

"Then what are y'all gonna do?"

"Get on our bellies on the ground, and start pumping lead into that wagon."

"Then what am I gonna be doing?"

"Shooting fire arrows into the wagon."

"Okay guys what are all of you gonna do when the wagon catches on fire?"

Bud said, "Nothin' till they try to get out, then we're gonna kill every one of 'em."

"What is the most important thing you're gonna do after they are all down."

One of the guys said, "Go get the money."

"Alright now don't everybody go running up there getting in each other's way. The first guy who gets to the wagon get it open and start handing out the crates, form a bucket line each one passing the box back to the next guy until we get'em all, then get back and let the wagon burn to the ground."

"Remember guys that wagon is gonna be hauling close to two-hundred thousand dollars in it. I'm gonna take half but that still leaves about twenty-thousand dollars for each of you. It would take you fifty years to earn that much working as a cow hand. You could go to Dallas or San Francisco and live like a king with that much money."

Bud said, "I still don't think it's right you gettin' half, all by yourself."

"Bud, if you want to you can quit right now and get on your horse and ride away. Your horse better be able to out run a bullet from this Winchester because we ain't leavin' no witnesses. That is why you're gonna shoot the driver because that way if this goes bad and we get caught, you're gonna hang right alongside the rest of us."

Bud starred at Jud for a minute then said, "I guess I'm just gettin' grouchy twenty thousand is a lot of money."

"Okay everybody get in position, keep them rifle barrels down until you're ready to start shootin' we don't want any sun light reflecting off a gun barrel and give them any warning."

Ronnie had the three teams hitched up ready to go when Grady walked out. He pulled out his watch and looked at it. "Six-thirty, they'll be coming around that bend in about ten minutes if they're on time." He glanced around and saw that everybody that was supposed to go on this run was standing by.

The two men from the railroad walked up and one of them said, "Well Grady this is a historic day."

"I hope it is a long boring day. It's gonna be a long day anyway," Grady said.

Someone in the crowd said, "There it comes." They all heard two long blasts from the train horn as it rounded the bend one mile east of the depot.

With the screech of metal brakes and hiss of steam the train ground to a stop. "Move the wagon Ronnie, let's get this loaded."

Ronnie guided the three teams pulling the wagon to the side of the baggage car. A man in a railroad guard uniform slid the side door open and two other men started handing crates down to the men in the wagon. The loading took only a few minutes. The man in the guard uniform handed Grady a manifest for him to sign, "Well it's your responsibility now. We got it this far, good luck. That's a heavy load you 're carrying."

The two railroad men stepped up and shook Grady's hand, good luck guys.

Colleen was on her knees praying,

Oh God what did I get Grady into?

It seemed so simple when we agreed to it. The money they were going to pay was so much.

Lord I beg you to watch over those men today. Please don't let any harm come to them. Make this be just another freight delivery day.

Amen

⇥⊹ ⊹⇤

Ronnie was driving. He wanted to stand up and drive standing so he could see better but Grady insisted that he stay down even if he couldn't see as well as he was used to.

One of the guys said "Jud here they come. They got two deputies riding with them."

"Remember now nobody fires until Bud takes that driver out. Then you two on this side shoot those deputies first."

Ronnie was just guiding the lumbering wagon up the grade from the dry creek bed when Bud opened fire. Ronnie slumped in the seat. Grady looked and saw all six mules fall in their traces. It sounded like a hundred guns opened up at the same time.

Grady saw a puff of gun smoke in front and to the right and sent a bullet right back to it. He saw a man rise up and fall back. Then the sound of gun fire was deafening. Guns were firing at the wagon and guns were firing from the wagon, it was deafening.

The men in the wagon couldn't see anybody to shoot at. Grady was yelling, "Aim for the gun smoke."

The men in the wagon could hear lead bullets hitting the sides of the wagon.

All at once they heard a loud thud as something different hit the side of the wagon. Grady looked out the port hole and his heart almost stopped. The thing that hit the wagon had bounced off and he saw what it was, it was a flaming arrow. As he watched he saw the trail of fire arching through the air toward the wagon. They were trying to set the wagon on fire.

He took quick aim and shot the arrow in flight knocking it off course. The fight took on a sense of desperation. Bullets were slamming into the boards on the side of the wagon, men in the wagon were firing at any gun smoke they could see. Grady was trying desperately to shoot the arrows down before they could hit the wagon and set the wooden box on fire turning it into a funeral pyre for the men in side.

The battle raged on. The men in the wagon noticed that only one rifle was now firing at them from the south side. All at once an arrow head punched through the wood on the top of the wagon box. Grady pushed the end of the barrel of his Winchester up to the end of the arrow and fired. The blast knocking the arrow head back out through the hole. They could see that the wood around the hole was on fire. Grady whipped his rifle around and using the butt of the rifle knocked a hole in the board forming the roof. Grabbed a canteen and sloshed water on to the flames starting to grow on the roof. That fire was out, but now they had a two foot hole in the roof. The next flaming arrow might come through the hole and land in one of the boxes of amination they had in the wagon. That would be real bad.

Over the noise of battle the men in the wagon heard another man cry out, as a bullet aimed at his gun smoke found its mark.

Jud realized his plan was not working, somebody in that wagon was shooting down his arrows as fast as he could lob them and the only one that had stuck and started fire they had been able to put out. Bud and the other two on the south side were either dead or they had deserted him.

All at once he saw a man jump down from the wagon and take cover behind a dead mule and start working his way forward moving from behind one dead mule to the other. Then a second man jumped down behind a dead mule.

"Little John, let's get out of here. They are trying to flank us."

Three outlaws raced to their horses and spurred the animals savagely to get away. Leaving three horses tied belonging to the three who would not be needing them anymore.

Grady walked over to the three horses left by the outlaws then he spied the two horses the deputies had been riding grazing nearby. "Guys let's get those mules out of the harness and hitch up these five horses to the wagon. We'll load the two deputies on board and the rest of us can walk if we have to, we've got a delivery to make and we'll leave the bodies of the deputies at the next town."

Pointing at the slain outlaws, someone asked, "What about them?"

"Leave'em for the coyotes. They don't deserve a Christian burial."

A somber group of freight men, one driving, the rest walking carrying Winchesters in their hands slowly proceeded to Beard.

Colleen walked into the lawyer's office, "Colleen did you hear that they're gonna arrest Jud this morning for the murder of your father?"

"No, did you say they're gonna arrest him this morning?"

"As soon as they can find him."

"I thought they couldn't prove it was him."

"The marshal and the sheriff went back to doc's house and searched it again, from top to bottom and they found the missing gold nugget wedged between the mattress and the headboard. I'm sorry it doesn't bring your father back but it does bring the ranch back to you."

"What? I don't understand."

"He filed that claim after he killed your father, so it's worthless. I'll file a motion with the court on your behalf to have the ranch returned to you and Marlene immediately. The court probably won't rule on it until after the trial and he's found guilty."

"Unbelievable. What will happen to Jud?"

"That's up to the court, but the jury will probably vote to see him hung because of the cowardly way he did it."

"Would I be a terrible person if I said I wanted to watch him hang?"

"No, I think you are entitled."

"I'm going to go over to the telegraph office and send a wire to Marlene."

As she walked out of his office Joe Thacker thought, Colleen is a very comely woman. If she weren't my client I would pursue courting her. Of course how can a young lawyer find a wife if not among his clients?

⊱ ⊰

It was almost dark when the last crate was off loaded at the bank In Buffalo Gap

"Guys' it's been a long day for all of us. I feel real bad about those two deputies. I'm gonna talk to Colleen and see what we can do to help their families. Lonnie how is Ronnie doing?"

"We are gonna get the doc to look at him but I think the bullet just grazed his hard head and he'll probably be alright. Gonna have a new part in his hair, and a head ache for a while."

CHAPTER SIXTY-SIX

All three outlaws looked as the sheriff, the marshal and eight deputies swept into the yard with guns drawn.

"What do you think you're doing? This is private property."

"Everybody keep your hands where we can see 'em. These men have orders to shoot the first man who even looks like he might be going for a gun. Jud you are under arrest for murder."

"What, are you crazy?"

The sheriff motioned to two deputies, "gather up all the guns. Marshal would you like to do the honor?"

"I sure would, he stepped off his horse and clamped the iron cuffs on Jud's hands."

The sheriff looked at Jud's men and said, "Boys ya'll have got a horse. I suggest you get on it and ride out of my county because if you're still here in five minutes. I'm gonna lock each one of you up until I can find out if you're wanted anywhere."

"Can we at least have our guns back?"

Turning to the deputy that had picked up the guns he said, "Shuck all of the shells out of 'em and give'em back." Then he turned his attention back to the men, "Don't even think about re-loading until you are well away from here."

Jud said. "This is preposterous you can't tie me to no murder."

The marshal reached in his shirt pocket and pulled out a big gold nugget and held it in the palm of his hand. Look what we found wedged between the mattress and the head board of the bed Mr. O'Shanity was murdered in."

CHAPTER SIXTY-SEVEN

As the empty wagon rumbled back home, Grady worried about Knot, *will I find the old dog dead when I get home? I hope not' I like old Knot.*

After they unhooked the teams, Grady thanked each one of the brave men who went out on the line with him. He then headed for his apartment, he almost dreaded what he might find when he got there.

Grady eased into the dark room and lit a lamp then carried the lamp over to Knot's bed. He jumped back "What the devil's that?" He leaned a little closer and shook his head, there was something else in that bed. He squinted his eyes and looked closer. "How in the world?" Then he started to laugh out loud, "six puppies were in there with Knot, why Knot, you ain't no he, you're a she. No wonder you've been moping around lately."

"Wait until I tell Marlene about this."

www.ingramcontent.com/pod-product-compliance
Lightning Source LLC
Chambersburg PA
CBHW051630260626
47170CB00004B/1121